CONQUERING THE POWER OF DEATH

A Vietnam survival story

DAVID LEE FOSTER

authorHOUSE®

AuthorHouse™
1663 Liberty Drive
Bloomington, IN 47403
www.authorhouse.com
Phone: 1-800-839-8640

This is a work of fiction. Any similarity of characters to actual persons living or dead is merely coincidental. While the author's personal experiences are reflected and due effort has been given to accurately recognize the dates, times, and places of certain national and world events, any truths asserted are subjective and simply constitute the author's vision and imagination of how those events transpired, if at all. The author was a Sergeant with the United States Marine Corps and did serve in Vietnam circa 1970.

Published by AuthorHouse 3/20/2012

ISBN: 978-1-4685-5875-3 (sc)
ISBN: 978-1-4685-5876-0 (hc)
ISBN: 978-1-4685-5877-7 (e)

Library of Congress Control Number: 2012903969

**Dedicated to all Reconnaissance Marines
who served in Vietnam
and to all Navy-Marine Corps MARS radio operators who
brought moments of joy to countless others
both state-side and in Vietnam.**

"Semper Fi" Marines

http://www.1streconbnassociation.org/

http://www.marinecorpsmars.com/

CONTENTS

"You would know the secret of death.
But how shall you find it unless you seek it in the heart of life?"

Kahlil Gibran, <u>The Prophet</u>

THE TRUTH OF THE MATTER

The local veterans sat in folding chairs lining the curb, waiting for the lead elements of the Memorial Day Parade to reach them, some were old, some quite young. The conversation was about "which war" and how many from the local area survived or died. The rumble of drums from a marching band became ever louder.

As the open top car carrying a D-Day survivor of Omaha Beach passed by, a 60ish Marine Vietnam Veteran removed his hat and saluted the former corporal. The D-Day survivor recognized the standing Marine as his former newspaper boy from 50 years back and proudly sat up straight in the car and saluted back, his heart bursting with pride.

One of the WWII vets, seeing the salute, said "He was not in the first wave at Omaha you know; he was a clerk in the rear". When no response came from the Marine, the WWII vet asked "Did you serve at the front in Vietnam?" Getting no response again, the WWII vet spoke to the other vets and said "Well at least we won our war!" One of the Vietnam vets hearing the comment responded: "We gave better than we got old man, at least the names of our dead fit on a Wall - and Charlie knows that". The Marine winced but said nothing as his mind drifted back to Vietnam, a forty-two year old memory that he had recalled just last night – like every other night. The 'Nam…..

* * * * *

Ever present danger was assuaged by monotonous routine; you just knew nothing was going to happen "in the rear". But after being lulled into complacency like a youth with no fear of mortality, something always did happen; hindsight always prevailed to lend credibility to the ubiquitous danger. The contradiction just oozed irony, and blood. Strange it was that one feared death at the "front" and survived, only to be seduced by the security of the "rear" and killed; thus were rules of engagement turned into a fool's agenda. Truth told, the only practical rules of engagement in Vietnam sounded in the ways of survival, not written or detailed but rather, sensed and absorbed as some airborne inoculation.

How many American soldiers were lost trying to pull villagers, usually woman and children, out of underground holes in huts and "hooches" rather than simply dropping a white phosphorous grenade in to ensure everyone had already come out and that there were no enemy? Would that the media cover the deaths of three Marines from an underground suicide sapper with the same intensity that they filmed the burned and scared bodies of innocent woman and children in the earthen hole!

And how many Corpsmen and medical aircraft personnel perished in failed "dust-off" operations while removing the dead and dying from the battlefield? And how many caches of rice, food for an entire village, exploded when the contents were sifted for the presence of weapons and, in doing so, thereby killed more Marines? In Hue City alone, how many civilians were shamelessly used as human shields by retreating elements of Viet Cong who had simply been interrupted in their mass killing of the Old Imperial City's upper class by advancing U.S. Marines? The subsequent discovery of mass graves lined with decomposing lime spoke volumes of the Viet Cong's murderous intent.

Against this backdrop, the practical rules of engagement increasingly amounted to survival. More pointedly, the real enemy was in the North and the ground war was in the South and the lines of resupply were located in the contiguous countries of Laos and Cambodia; both venues were beyond the jurisdictional rules of engagement of ground forces except in rare instances.

CONQUERING THE POWER OF DEATH

In light of neglect or refusal to fully engage the enemy in a meaningful fashion, a form of expediency came to the engagement process much like a bastardization of the local language into pithy phrases of part-Vietnamese, part-French, and part vulgarity. In time, in a very short time for a grunt in the field, the notion of survival meant gleaning unspoken and unwritten rules into their daily conduct in an effort to survive. And the stricter and more pronounced the rules of engagement (such as those "in the rear"), the more adaption of those rules gave rise to survival.

And as with all rules in a military operation, the lower one's rank the less discretion was accorded the soldier. An officer's improvising, overcoming, and adapting was found in a different universe than a mere private's effort to do the same. Yet the likelihood of the need for adaption was most peculiarly at the point of the spear, that is, the grunt in the field. And so, the young, inexperienced, just in from "the world" grunt, probably around 19 years old, would confront a life or death situation with the result being his own death or someone else's death. Death had a way of covering all its bases to insure that, in one way or another, it would win.

Thus was it that the mission to win Vietnamese "hearts and minds" turned to a bunker-mentality undertaking of "us" against "them", and in that moment, in that knowledge, in that survival mode was Vietnam lost: not in some major battle, not in some strategic operation, but in the day to day quest for continued existence and survival. The profound sadness was not in our losing an armed conflict but rather, in death's ability to seemingly stilt the psyche both during and after one's tour of duty.

That same monotonous routine gave definition to homesickness, a pining for the time a thirteen month "tour of duty" would elapse so that one could return home to loved ones and to the "world". Everyone, it seemed, had a short-timer's calendar setting forth how many days one had left "in the 'Nam"! In the interim, communication with home took the form of writing letters, recording cassette tapes, and connecting telephonically through something called "phone patches" via Ham or Amateur radio in places called MARS Stations.

The common denominator for monotonous routine and homesickness

3

was a loathing for the possible ultimate consequence of a tour of duty in Vietnam: death. It did not escape those involved in Vietnam that death is not one of life's options, so the sooner it happened in life, the more tragic it became.

Aside from death not coming where and when one would expect it in Vietnam, there remained the "how"; death could be so much more than dying, as when one longs for an end to living. That is when death no longer is the opposite of birth but rather, an undefined state of existence wherein one is neither alive nor deceased. Such was the enigma of not coming back from Vietnam in the same mental state as when one arrived and such was the persona of death in Vietnam. Doctors and professionals, it seemed, could correctly diagnose the problem generically as a "head wound" but their treatment protocol for this type of "wound" was akin to placing a tourniquet around the neck!

But what kind of a "head wound" encompassed the duality of logic and rational fear, even irrational fear? Few understood and even fewer comprehended with appreciation, the war zone mindset. The stream of consciousness of a nineteen year old grunt engaged in combat was an excursion into madness, loyalty, and profound courage.

"We are Marines, mess with the best, die like the rest" seemed to be an ego boosting anthem played by bulletproof young warriors.

"I cannot be a coward among my fellow Marines; if they can do it, so can I." encompassed many a grunt's inward thoughts and fears.

"We are the tip of the spear for our country; let them try to attain their Điện Biên Phủ with us. We are not French", spoke brave and dedicated warriors.

"Who will care if I die on Hill 861, a place so important they did not even name it, they only measured its height. And looking down from the victorious top there is nothing, nothing at all of value here" murmured and mumbled many a grunt.

"These poor people need someone to protect them, to simply let them live in peace and have their children know security" spoke many a Marine's heart.

"How can we protect people who won't fight for themselves? How do I know they are not really the enemy? My only concern is my fellow Marine" pondered a host of troops.

"Marines can endure whatever it takes to get the job done. I promise to give my enemy every opportunity to die for his country" boasted some Marines.

"And what will my death prove, or change, or even mean? I do not care about these people; I only care about my fellow Marine" surmised more than one Marine's heart.

And against this frame of mind sat Death, unfathomable, unplumbed, and immeasurable Death; perched on the brink of humanity's sanity for a clear eye view of a human's descent into the abyss. Death, with ions and millennia of experience brought to bear against youthful notions of patriotism, naïve political belief, and green, adolescent resolve was clearly in charge save some modicum of faith and reliance upon goodness. Yet even Death feared faith but seldom found enough of it to genuflect and depart. And so a "head wound" was all of this, and more. How could one explain a "head wound" when it was virtually impossible to find the words to describe it? Perhaps the neck tourniquet was the correct remedy.

In the end, a "head wound" resulting from death's grip found no panacea, no cure, no antibiotic, and no pain management; it simply bred irony that what could have happened did not, and what was unlikely to occur in fact did, with the net effect that a person's life was changed forever - and that was the painful truth of the matter.

CHAPTER I

THE SITUATION

D a Nang, Vietnam, today situated in the mid-coastal region, was "the rear" in early 1970, so much so that some Marines stationed there resided in "hooches" and even outside secured access compounds. Although there was a First Marine Division Compound and a First Marine Air Wing Compound, one could walk or hitch a ride to "Freedom Hill USO" or go across the airfield to the Fleet Air Support Unit (FASU) clubs for a burger, fries, pizza, or cheap alcoholic drinks, paid for in funny money called Military Payment Certificates or MPC. Some upscale hooches even had air conditioners and small refrigerators. Yet the weapons of war were never far away: a K-bar knife strapped to the body, a 45 pistol on the hip, an M-79 grenade launcher over the shoulder or an M-16 with multiple clips ready to be clutched - and always a bunker of sand bags close by. Death could still come quickly though by rocket or mortar or sapper or simply murder. But Da Nang was also home to Camp Reasoner, the First Marine Division Reconnaissance Compound, and helicopters unceremoniously delivered groups of six to eight Marines to and from the "boonies" for reconnaissance and death: sometimes Marines', sometimes the enemy's, but always death.

The juxtaposition of troops behind enemy lines or those deployed to no-man's land for brief periods of time with camps "in the rear" was unique to Vietnam because of the helicopter. A mere glance at the bottleneck topography of the 1970's boundary between South and North Vietnam provides insight into just how quick one could be "in the rear" one minute and "in the boonies" the next. Insertion or deployment to a nearby hill or valley could be a short helicopter ride away. But the relative security of one world (base camp) and the high, almost suicidal, risk of a hilltop a few miles away made for a roller coaster ride of emotions.

Fear, anxiety, and death could literally be a few minutes flight time away. At one moment, reconnaissance troops could be isolated, endangered, outnumbered, and on the defensive only to be "in the rear" and sleeping in a tent a few moments and a helicopter ride later - of such extremes are trauma manifested. The arduous task of reconnaissance required young, fit soldiers most likely lacking in the one thing that could make some life saving sense out of this flip-flop existence: emotional maturity. But if "necessity is the mother of invention", recon troops learned quickly to improvise, overcome, and adapt both physically, mentally, and spiritually, no matter what their age, to invent maturity.

Against this backdrop one could find nineteen-year-old, young-looking warriors, grunts and recon types who, notwithstanding their youth, were highly skilled fighters, truly feared and respected by even accomplished, battle-hardened NVA soldiers and dogma dedicated Viet Cong. That they were kids back in the "world", either going to college, working at some job, or just hanging out was of little moment; in the 'Nam they were an occupying force, the tip of the spear, and hence targets.

While certainly no where as dangerous as reconnaissance duties, radio duties for those assigned with MARS stations normally consisted of personnel being located off compounds and in secluded areas; so much so that getting to a mess hall, a club, or to any secure military installation involved unprotected travel and unprotected in Vietnam could mean ambush and death.

For example, living off a compound meant inherent risks in the early movement of an offensive, as the occupants of the American Embassy in Saigon found out during Tet, 1968. Although the embassy was guarded and constituted its own fenced in area, it was not a military base other than the presence of a few Marine guards, and a force of mixed American and Vietnamese military police. It lacked the operational security of a normal combat base with perimeters located within perimeters.

And travel to and from anywhere, whether emptying the trash, going to the PX, or simply leaving the radio station to go somewhere in the rear, was unlikely to include packing an arsenal and body armor – possibly a fatal mistake.

So it was that a simple walk to get a burger, perhaps even in civilian clothes, or a benign jaunt through the jungle to "the rear" to gather supplies might turn into a fight-for-your-life-survival odyssey. And the mistrust born of that scenario forever extinguished a genuine search for the enemy's heart and mind; the search rather was to know when and where to locate the enemy's head and center body mass with one, if not two, shots.

By contrast, those fighting on the front lines or in the trenches were understandably dismissive of a "fear in the rear" syndrome. While being on patrol, setting an ambush, or pointedly being on a search and destroy mission had its own grave dangers and attendant risks, the milieu, by its very nature, heightened awareness and brought the full force of arms to bear against the enemy. Death was real and could be expected as surely as a weekly body count of U.S. casualties. Rotation off the front lines, stand down time, and switching out individuals, even platoons, from repetitive duties all insured a sharing of risks while still keeping troops in the field. And even though the gun may have been locked and loaded, the enemy was not sighted in during such times; hence a form of false respite existed where the lull was an anticipatory one. The proof of this is that those troops were regularly given an in-country R&R to places like Da Nang and China Beach!

The sad truth was that death happened in the rear, it was still "the 'Nam" and death was in attendance; that was the reality - the real situation.

CHAPTER II

THE MARINES OF RECONNAISENCE TEAM EAGLE

Bone-rack was a 120 pound, nineteen year old Marine Lance Corporal from upstate New York, so-called because he looked like an emaciated, scrawny rack of bones. The Lance Corporal was not male-nourished by any means, just 5'8" of not so muscular Marine. But the gaunt teenager had a talent: he could direct artillery or call in an airstrike with precise coolness even in the midst of a raging battle, he could read a map, determine coordinates, and have the courage and conviction to rain hell down upon enemy just meters away. The other Marines wanted Bone-rack with them on patrol because very few had the courage to carry a twenty-three pound PRC 25 radio on their back and fewer still could use that radio deftly and efficiently to deliver death to the enemy. And oh yes, as a radio buff, a so-called Ham radio operator since his early teens, Bone-rack's part time job in the rear was to run "phone patches" though a military radio station back to the "world", a free call home to loved ones. Knowing Bone-rack often meant a ticket to calling home while "in the rear" and, at times, even in the field through the use of a PRC25 and radio relay.

Pig man's moniker, on the other hand, was no allusion to the young, native Pennsylvanian Marine's appetite, physique or sexual proclivities but rather, to his military occupational specialty or MOS. A 0331 MOS

Marine carried a twenty-three pound M-60 machine gun that delivered a 7.62mm round hundreds of times a minute, usually from the center of an ambush. The pig man cleaned up the mess of enemy fire; he ate up everything that was left of a charging enemy - hence the descriptive name. And other than the radio man, he was ordinarily one of the first targeted in an ambush so as to deny the enemy force's firepower. As if Pig man needed any further liking by his fellow Marines, he just happened to be charged with laying down a devastating deluge of fire against the enemy so that others could re-group and carry out a counter-attack. The M-60 was not a usual weapon for a fast moving reconnaissance team but had found a place due to this particular team's specialized missions. It meant other team members carried extra ammo for Pig man.

Bone-rack and Pig man had much in common on Reconnaissance Team Eagle: they each humped twenty-three pounds of gear in addition to their own belongings and no one wanted their jobs yet everyone wanted their presence - preferably in good working order. They had something else in common: both Lance Corporals were 19 and had killed several enemy soldiers over their short time "in the 'Nam" with their specialized gear: Bone-rack with a radio and Pig man with a machine gun. And each knew his job well.

Bankhead, the lone Black on Reconnaissance Team Eagle, was a veteran of many wars: the racial one in his head, the south-side Chicago shithole he survived to get to the 'Nam, the prior battles of Vietnam which earned him his Sergeant stripes, and the personal one he fought daily to understand just who he was. He was a curious devotee of Malcolm X, Muhammad Ali, and Martin Luther King; two were dead – murdered - and the survivor had firmly stated that no Viet Cong had ever called him "Nigger". But Bankhead was also a Marine, and a Sergeant at that; the inner turmoil could not have been more apparent. But to the other team members of Eagle, he was not a Black Marine, a Black Sergeant, or a Black anything, he was "Sarge" and that meant everything to him. To Bone-rack and Pig man Sarge was a larger than life "reconner", even if he was only two years older. And neither Bone-rack nor Pig man knew much, if anything, of Malcolm X, Muhammad Ali, or Martin Luther King – maybe that one was a boxer, maybe.

LT, or the Lieutenant, was not 19 but a crusty 25 and on his second Vietnam tour. He was also a trained forward observer for spotting artillery, air, and naval gunfire. An Ivy League graduate from New England, he was prone to reading books the titles of which those around him could not quite discern or even pronounce. As if it were possible, a Lieutenant's life span in combat was rumored to be even shorter than the radioman or M60 gunner, even if only by a shot or two. LT was respected by his troops for he led by example but, unlike Bone-rack and Pig man, was someone who could order other Marines to their deaths by simply assigning duties, a trait which set less well with him than his troops. Team Eagle believed in him perhaps more than he believed in himself and Sarge knew it. LT had a penchant, though, for knowing his men and seeing things in them that others or even the men themselves did not or could not see. He saw ability and accomplishment, doubt and faith, and, oh yes, he saw good and bad. He saw these things and he knew that precious knowledge had been entrusted to him by some higher force - he was indeed the poet warrior. LT had so much going for him: his Ivy League credentials, his leadership, his acceptance by his underlings, that to die in Vietnam would be a huge and poignant loss; his classical education painfully reminded him that such was the anatomy of a tragedy - and war, an essential ingredient, was an overpowering force.

Ricky recon was a Macon, Georgia good ole boy that, if you believed him, had a member of his family fight in every war since the American Revolution. He had received formal training after Marine Corps boot camp in reconnaissance, hence the name Ricky recon. Gregarious by nature, he was the life of any party, especially one in a war zone, but, truly and ironically, his heart was known to none as they say. What was known amounted to a consensus; everyone was glad he was not on the other side. Large in stature and viscerally tough, he made an imposing point man for Team Eagle. A bit older than the rest of the team members at 30, and a staff non-commissioned officer (SNCO), he was what the troops called a "lifer" meaning that he made the Marine Corps his profession. If he could not be part of the Marine Corps, he just was not sure where he would fit in, if at all. LT looked up to Ricky recon which is another way of saying Ricky recon looked down on LT. Perhaps it explained why a senior NCO walked point while the higher ranking LT brought up the rear; or perhaps not – it was one of those 'Nam things and besides, Sarge walked wherever he wanted to. That was fine with Ricky recon, he only saw Sarge through Marine Corps green tinted glasses. For their part, Bone-rack and Pig man always wanted to be sure that LT's orders coincided with what Ricky recon or Sarge thought appropriate. No one wanted to envision a situation where the three did not agree on a course of action because it would have been difficult, if not impossible, to follow what the NCO's said instead of LT's direction. This was not a disparagement of LT, just a grunt thing - Marine Corps NCOs and SNCOs were the glue that made "Esprit De Corps" the sticky thing it was.

Other members of the strike force came and went as rotations back to the "world" occurred. Be they fire team members or forward observers along for the ride, they were still part of the team in the field, but the team was not always part of them in the rear.

What everyone was an integral part of, however, was the TRAP team known only as Eagle: a Tactical Recovery of Aircraft and Personnel unit. In simple terms, pilots and crew went up and sometimes were forced to come down in unplanned areas. The TRAP unit assured their recovery, dead or alive, by being inserted as a group by helicopter, finding their "package", and returning safely to base with all. At times, it was a deadly game of cat-and-mouse with a ruthless, committed, and determined enemy. After all, the enemy were nationalists on their home turf and the Marines travelled thousands of miles to get there as an occupying force. Team Eagle may have been disadvantaged by being on the enemy's ground and always numerically outnumbered, but the team had access to superior airpower and firepower and, the team members liked to think, superior skills. It was no mistake that the TRAP unit had a lieutenant, a staff NCO, and yet another NCO; the mission was a specialized one and required different talents and varied authority.

LT, as a forward observer, could coordinate close air support with the air wing or call up specialized firepower like naval gunfire. Ostensibly, a trained officer lent a measure of insurance and accuracy to this highly complex art-form of coordinating the trajectory of naval gunfire and the closeness of air or artillery support. In the heat of battle, however, the radioman became the nexus between the trained officer's directions and ordinance provider. But when the officer was otherwise engaged in the battle itself, the onus of obtaining firepower often fell upon the on-site radioman. And sometimes, there was no ability to communicate at all, as when the team itself was simply engaged in stealth, evasion, or escape.

There was a time when over four hundred NVA regulars simply walked over the top of a highly concealed and extraordinarily evasive Team Eagle in the still of night only to find deadly ordinance rained down on them at first light - a feat which brought praise for each team member's accomplishments. The evasion, the deadly artillery barrage, the expertly led plan, and the courage of all buried in the undergrowth as deadly, booted and sandaled feet walked over them, spoke volumes of the team's cunning and ability. Not a shot was fired, not a man was lost; the team carried their package to the extraction point and then inflicted literally hundreds of deaths upon an unsuspecting enemy.

Somewhere in the waning moments before daylight, the teenagers became older, the package became a believer, LT found himself forever indebted to God for delivering his men safely, and, while Ricky recon cast a slightly higher glance at LT, he continued to insist that if the unit had been discovered there would still be four hundred dead NVA; Sarge knew better – miracles rarely, if ever, happened on the south side of anywhere, be it Vietnam or Chicago.

And somewhere in the moments after Team Eagle's reprieve, Death looked back up the hill and promised to return; Team Eagle needed no reminder, each member was acutely aware of Death's presence. But Sarge also knew these Marines were a cut above the rest; they were, in fact, the Marines of Reconnaissance Team Eagle.

CHAPTER III

MARINES FROM MARS

MARS, or more appropriately, Navy-Marine Corps Military Affiliate Radio System, was an irregular group of communication specialists engaged with their civilian counterparts in phone and message traffic to and from the troops and "the world". Early on in the Vietnam Conflict, the Marine Corps sought to harness the skills of Ham or Amateur Radio Operators within its ranks to form an alliance with volunteer hams for the purpose of providing communication between the troops and their loved ones at home.

The organization was "irregular" in the sense that the normal chain of command was all but dispensed with in favor of first names, off-base or off-compound radio stations, the wearing of predominately civilian clothes instead of uniforms, and a very close camaraderie between the operators. In essence, MARS members thought of themselves and their civilian counterparts more as family than members of a military unit or quasi-military operation, often to the consternation of the normally tradition poised Marine Corps. Master Sergeants, privates, corporals, lieutenants, and even an occasional general, worked in close proximity to one another on a first name basis as ham radio operators more than as Marines.

At the height of the Vietnam Conflict virtually every Marine Corps base had a MARS station as did every Marine Corps compound in

Vietnam. Da Nang, Chu Lai, An Hoa, Marble Mountain, Phu Bai, and even the hospital ships U.S.S. Sanctuary and U.S.S. Repose in the South China Sea had stations. The sole purpose was morale of the troops and "as instant" communication as was possible given the technology of the time; it was about as close to a phone call as one could get.

Nearly all the MARS Marines shared two common traits: an amateur radio license back in the states and the hobby of Ham Radio. And the Marine Corps provided the MARS Marines with the latest in communication gear: the so-called Collins S-Line of transmitters and receivers, Henry linear Amplifiers, and state of the art antenna systems. Most Marine commands had little notion of what MARS did, only that they provided an essential service to the troops and were headquartered in Washington, D.C. In essence, Marine commands left MARS to carry out its mission with as little intervention or oversight as possible.

From the outside, it appeared that those assigned to MARS operations were sacred cows; MARS personnel normally lived off the compound, were engaged in their own chain of command, and with the exception of core Marine Corps requirements like rifle qualification or physical fitness requirements, were exempt from most other obligations such as mess or guard duty, at least most of the time. They also seemed to have rather nice quarters: their own rooms, air conditioners, and the ability to come and go as they pleased to accommodate their "radio schedules". In essence, it was sweet duty. Being sent to Vietnam "for duty with MARS" often meant specialized treatment.

In Vietnam, some of that detachment from military routine became, at times, problematic. Because of the antenna systems – tall steel towers – the stations were not normally located on a compound. And because of equipment needs for temperature controlled environments, the stations were usually air conditioned. Since the stations were off the compounds, the MARS personnel normally took their meals at the station and were therefore allowed refrigerators and cook tops, usually gleaned from barter with other units. It did not take a genius to figure out that MARS duty was unlike military duty in many ways.

But Death, either by concept or event, was no stranger to MARS.

If a Marine lost a loved one at home, a phone call was the quickest communication to make arrangements or to convey condolences. Being part of any such communication brought involvement in another's issues, in another's life, and it also brought the notion of death closer; a force that one wanted to keep at bay in a war zone. To be sure, the vast majority of phone patches and message traffic were upbeat, positive, and morale boosting. But when the situation warranted compassion, assistance, and understanding, MARS personnel were there to help.

Additionally, the ever present thought of being off a regular compound conjured up death's potential. Although it never actually happened that MARS personnel were killed at a station, the point was, it could have happened.

And so while MARS duty was certainly better than most Vietnam assignments, it was not without it drawbacks or complications; most would say, however, that any threat of physical danger paled in comparison to other assignments.

Living and working in such close proximity brought life long friendships and intense, tight relationships. A thirteen month tour very often yielded close bonding between the operators and a genuine penchant for helping troop morale. Working with the latest equipment was like providing a grease monkey a new Corvette; it just did not get any better.

When MARS personnel found other ham radio operators among the troops, the connection was instant. Bone-rack, a ham radio operator and a radioman had been sent to Vietnam "for duty with MARS" from a stateside base but, as military logistics is want to do, found that other things happened to co-op that direction.

A normal day of phone patches and written teletype messages was far from boring. Having a radio operator on each end of the communication meant listening to the same colloquy but always with a twist, some humorous, some poignant.

A funny phone patch exchange occurred when a young Lieutenant on his way to R&R advised his lover who was to meet him there that she should be sure to have a mattress strapped to her when he arrived.

Her unexpected retort that he better be the first man off the plane drew howls of laughter.

A poignant phone patch exchange grew out of a highly emotional grunt telling his brother that he just did not think he would make it back alive and then began crying; it was gut wrenching to hear such emotional turmoil. Somehow, maintaining the Vietnam side of the conversation was always more pointed as the operator not only could hear the soldier speak but see the emotions first hand.

While a MARS station is where Bone-rack was supposed to go in Vietnam and while it is where he ended up, it only occurred by taking the long way around the barn. Ultimately, MARS would save Bone-rack's life. The Marines from MARS did find him and eventually bring him back onboard. It was not the first time a hobby altered or saved one's life. The Marines from MARS were there for Bone-rack when he needed them most.

CHAPTER IV

SIX MONTHS EARLIER

Bone-rack arrived in Vietnam shortly after his 19th birthday after more than a year of active duty Marine Corps training. Exiting the commercial jetliner on the tarmac at the sprawling Da Nang airbase, his first observations were the intense heat of the afternoon sun and the constant state of confusion. No one knew exactly where to go and it seemed that everyone was milling around. The officers were quickly whisked away by jeeps or by couriers and the senior enlisted men seemed to slowly find direction. The troops stood around in the midday sun gathering their canvass sea bags. All the ground personnel seemed to be wearing T shirts and covers (hats in civilian parlance), while those just in from the "world" were still dressed in long sleeve, heavy cotton, green shirts. It was stifling and the absence of order made it more than a bit unnerving, even scary.

Someone with a manifest list finally showed up and directed the group inside a large building. As names were called, destinations were announced. Groups were then told to sit and wait for transportation which would be there "shortly". Now in military terms "shortly" is relative: before the end of the Vietnam Conflict, before the end of the day, before sundown, or before being transferred back to the "world" at the end of one's tour, were all possible candidates for "shortly". As it turned out, before sundown drew short straw and Bone-rack learned he was on his way to a fire support combat base called An Hoa, a base camp for the Fifth Marine Regiment. Although he had no clue at the time, An Hoa was about 18 miles south and slightly to the west of Da Nang and it was little more than sandbags, dust, confusion, and, oh yes, death. From that location the troops in the field could expect fire support from the 105 Howitzer canons, quick response troops, "med-evac" choppers, and little else in the way of amenities. The red earth and sandy dirt would have made a great horse trail ranch with a fantastic view in any other time and location. In 1970 Vietnam it was the tent city encased in sandbags that one saw – and those mountains on the horizon were simply where brave men died doing reconnaissance missions essential to the war effort. Ironically and very typically, those mountains were so strategic they had no names, just numbers representing their elevation above hell.

Although Bone-rack's orders clearly read "for duty with MARS Da Nang", meaning assignment to a MARS Radio Station in Da Nang, the burly Gunnery Sergeant simply said "saddle up" as they loaded onto the 6-by for transport to the far side of the airport for a helicopter ride to An Hoa, the only safe way to get there. And besides, a Lance Corporal would not question a Gunnery Sergeant; he just did what he was told.

A short time later, and almost dusk, the Sea Stallion helicopter was at the LZ in An Hoa. The other occupants of the helicopter moved fast to disembark and the booming 105 Howitzers made a convincing case for doing so; Bone-rack's first clue that this clearly was an operational base and that operations were going on. There were tents everywhere and as Bone-rack looked out at the surrounding hills he could see the perimeter laced with rolls of concertina wire. The crew chief pointed him towards an admin tent as Bone-rack realized no one stood around in the open; it was not healthy.

A processing clerk, another Lance Corporal, read Bone-rack's orders and concluded he was indeed a radioman; not a MARS Radio operator but rather, a radioman. "'Comm tent' is over there" he informed Bone-rack by pointing. Upon arriving at the "Comm tent" Bone-rack met another Lance Corporal. "Hi, I am Pig man" the Lance Corporal said "Get your 782 gear and let's go eat chow before it is gone" Pig man announced.

782 gear was a colloquialism for war gear; in this case, issuance of an M16 rifle, a helmet, a flack jacket, magazines of ammo, a bayonet, and field clothes. Pig man showed him an empty tent and Bone-rack threw his gear on the rack and started to go. Pig man pointed to the M16 and ammo: "You do not go anywhere without that, Mr. Radioman" he said; Bone-rack's second clue that they were, indeed, in the bush. As he started out again, Pig man picked up Bone-rack's flack jacket and helmet and tossed them at him: "It is a court martial offense to be without them out here dude" he matter-of-factly said. Bone-rack put them on and wondered just how he was supposed to know all these rules. On their way to the mess tent he asked Pig man just that question. Pig man laughed and said: "Because I just told you." "I am curious" Bone-rack said, "How did you get the nick name Pig man?" Pig man looked at Bone-rack intently and then said: "You really are just in from the 'world' aren't you! Pig man, as in machine gunner, as in the pig who cleans it all up, get it?" Bone-rack got it but just looked confused about the name. "And how about you, what do they call you besides Lance Corporal or radioman?" Pig man inquired. "Everyone calls me Bone-rack" Bone-rack said. Pig man laughed: "Well, it fits" he said, "shit; you look like a rack of bones." Of such exchanges were friends made in the 'Nam.

"So you are the new RTO (Marine speak for radio/telephone operator)?" asked Pig man. "Well not quite" replied Bone-rack, "yes I am a radioman but I am a MARS radio operator and I was supposed to be assigned to Da Nang." Pig man laughed: "Welcome to the 'Nam man" was all he said, not quite sure what a MARS radio operator was but certain that Bone-rack was now "their" radio operator by default.

Their meal was interrupted by a steadily screeching siren and instant commotion as everyone hit the deck. The whine of rockets was followed by thuds and the inevitable explosions shook the ground, then silence. Everyone filed out of the tent to see seriously wounded Marines being hurriedly carried away; someone said they would not make it. Meanwhile, Pig-man nonchalantly explained that if the siren went up and down it meant there were "zips in the wires", in other words, they were being attacked and overrun.

As they stood there, two stretchers went by with blood covered Marines. Pig man was unfazed but Bone-rack lowered his head, made the sign of the cross, and said a prayer for them. An officer came up and motioned to Pig man, "This the newbee?" he said. Pig man responded: "Yes LT". Then the officer spoke. "Hi, I am LT and you are?" Pig man interrupted and introduced them saying "LT, this is Bone-rack our new RTO, just in from the 'world'." LT had seen him make the sign of the cross and now looked into Bone-rack's clear, blue eyes. "That was nice of you, Marine" he said, "but get used to it. Death wins a lot here. Follow me son." They walked to LT's tent where Bone-rack was introduced to a Black NCO who insisted on being called Sarge and a Staff NCO who simply said: "They, and you, call me Ricky recon", he then put his hand out. Bone-rack shook his hand and noticed his obvious strength and the largeness of his hand; Ricky recon noted Bone-rack's youth and naïveté. LT said: "Bone-rack, we are all recon and part of a TRAP unit, we pick up pilots and flight crew and sometimes even the aircraft. It is dangerous work, but you are in good hands. As you probably know, we are volunteers. So if you do not want to be with us, you will simply be with the comm unit. We will train you. I see from your orders that you were assigned to the Da Nang MARS Station, but you are here now. We will get it straightened out, but right now you are our new RTO. Are you trained and did you go through staging at Camp Pendleton for combat RTO duties?" "Yes sir" Bone-rack responded immediately, "And I was top in my class for hitting coordinates" he added. "Good" said LT, "then you are it. You will go along with our other RTO for the next two weeks. Just follow us, do what we tell you, and be calm. Ok?" "Yes sir" snapped Bone-rack. "And knock off the sir, do not salute me because I do not want you telling the enemy I am an officer." "Yes, sir, I mean yes LT." stammered Bone-rack. "Good" said LT, "we go out on perimeter watch tomorrow at 1600. Get a PRC 25, meet up with your counterpart, and carry extra water and plenty of ammo." "Yes LT" Bone-rack replied, a little surer of himself this time. As he left, LT looked at Sarge and Ricky recon. "They call him Bone-rack, but there is something about him that I can not quite put my finger on; I watched him pray over our two casualties just a moment ago. He is what we need here." LT said. "Begging your pardon LT, but what we need is a no- bullshit RTO" said Ricky recon. Sarge silently agreed with LT, they did need "a good man" but he also agreed with Ricky recon, good meant other things too, like getting the job done right so they all lived.

When Bone-rack returned to his tent, Pig man said "You know, you are with the best group on the base, this is Team Eagle. And they meant it when they told you the names: that's LT, Ricky recon, and Sarge." He then added: "I sure hope you know how to use that fucking radio." "I know" said Bone-rack, "trust me, I know." Pig man, for his part, would wait to see before agreeing but hoped that Bone-rack was right. Pig-man knew that there was such a thing as being "dead right".

Over the next several months, Bone-rack showed he was a quick learner; he was good with the coordinates, and did not get flustered under fire. As the old RTO left and rotated back to the "world", Bone-rack worked into his position with ever increasing precision. So much so, that LT, Sarge, Pig man, and Ricky recon realized he had talent. Bone-rack also established communications with the Da Nang MARS Station and did a radio relay with the PRC 25 that allowed Marines in the field to get calls home. He was a hit with his fellow Marines. And Da Nang MARS was trying to get him back!

Bone-rack also worked with the recon radio operators; he arranged calls to the "world" for them as well, made friends with them, and learned to ply their procedures exactly. He took naturally to the radio procedures from all his days in Ham radio and also found he was a "natural" map reader. In time, he went out with some daily recon operatives and learned to put the two skills together.

But, those first few months were fraught with routine and inexperience. Standing perimeter watch was a precarious duty and a test of one's character. Not being experienced enough to be an RTO on a team with a long range mission and yet being a basic Marine rifleman meant standing guard duty on the camp's perimeter at night. One always had to know the "word", not some clandestine code name or arcane password, but the "word" as in, "here is the situation tonight Marine", or "this is what to expect Marine", or "here is the scoop for this night's watch". Death resulted from screwing up the "word"! So, knowing and understanding the "word" meant staying alive!

On one particular night, the word was that local VC were stealthily meeting up with uniformed NVA to coordinate insurgency. At around 3:00 am, the Sergeant of the guard slipped by Bone-rack's hole (position) to let him know that there had been movement and that any moving things out in front were not indigenous personnel but rather, the enemy and to fire at will. As if that was not cause to have adrenalin pumping, the earlier watch had lost a "hole" meaning that one deployed position had been overrun and the Marine killed, stabbed to death. Bone-rack knew the word: fire at will.

At about 4:15 am, Bone-rack peered through the night vision scope and saw three crouched figures carrying things in their hands. They were moving into the clearing from the tree line and then seemed to stand still facing his position. In the distance, Bone-rack could hear occasional firing and then silence. Carefully putting the three figures in the sights of his M-16, Bone-rack waited, barely able to breath. His apprehensions turned to fear and then to horror as the three figures bent over and were slowly making their way in his direction. They moved very slowly as if looking for something on the ground, perhaps mines or trip flares; it never occurred to Bone-rack they could be doing anything else. After waiting for what seemed an eternity, Bone-rack took very careful aim and BANG, BANG, dropped two of the figures. The third began to run but a final BANG brought him down as well. Then all was silent. Bone-rack's heart was racing; he had killed the enemy!

When first light came, the platoon sergeant hurriedly corralled the various listening posts together. Before Bone-rack could report anything, the platoon sergeant said they needed to pull back immediately. When they finally went off duty, no debriefing or reporting was done. Bone-rack did not know whether this was normal or unusual, only that he thought he should tell someone what happened. Bone-rack went to chow along with the others certain that he would be told what to do – so certain, that he said nothing.

LT sat in his hooch and thought about his troops, especially his new troops and Bone-rack in particular. He had watched Bone-rack grow in skill and he also observed the reverence he had for the wounded or dead, on either side. He had also seen him attend Mass when the Chaplin came; he was a rare one, LT thought. But precisely because he was so rare, LT also knew that death would haunt and stalk him more harshly than the others. Watching Bone-rack deftly declare coordinates, adjust fire, and move with precision at critical times, he thought: "What a tragedy it would be to lose this kid." His first impression had proven prophetically correct: there was something about him, a decency, a humility that put him at odds with his crass surroundings. He was stronger than death for death could not extinguish the goodness within him. But he wondered if Bone-rack really knew that, he doubted it. At any rate, he thought, Bone-rack was ready to join the team and he would tell him after morning chow; and he felt comfortable with his decision. But Bone-rack had to decide as well; he could choose to stay with comm as an RTO or volunteer for recon, no one was forced to be in recon!

The next morning, after morning chow, there was the normal report from command to the platoon sergeants and to the troops. It seemed three locals, a man, his wife, and their young son, were found in their rice paddy in the early morning hours; they had been doing their farming and were found shot to death - their farming tools lying next to them. The matter was being reviewed to determine if they had been executed by the NVA. They had no weapons, only farming implements, and were found in a newly planted paddy. Each had been shot once.

Bone-rack was trembling and near hysteria when LT said he wanted to see him for a moment. Bone-rack's eyes were wide with fear and his heart was pounding as LT explained he felt he had performed well enough to date that he could henceforth be the RTO for Team Eagle! Bone-rack just stared at the ground. LT, sensing hesitation, said "Look, I know you are a bit overwhelmed, but trust me, you are ready." With that LT walked away and Bone-rack went to the head to be sick; he never told anyone about the shooting and no one ever asked. Pig man saw him puking and jokingly said: "All night watch didn't agree with you?" Bone-rack did not answer and he no longer wanted to stand perimeter watch in the rear; recon became his way to be assigned permanently away from the comm unit. It was dangerous but he would not be alone!

But, "the shooting that did not happen" never left Bone-rack's soul. Like radioactive iodine, the knowledge Bone-rack held in his soul would forever course through his being and glow and have a radioactive "half-life" both physically and spiritually; "half-life", that was an appropriate term.

Anger, reflection, embarrassment, depression, and simple melancholy each had an opportunity to mingle with Bone-rack's homesickness and immaturity. Slowly, faith and resolve became pillars upon which Bone-rack would resolve the tension between naïveté and experience. To be naïve without being reckless and to be experienced without being jaded proved to be a challenge; like a chameleon, Bone-rack was changing in color to green, Marine Corps green; reckless and jaded aptly described the transition. And while Bone-rack took pride in his new found camouflaging ability, he remembered acerbically that chameleons were lizards. Little did Bone-rack know that was another appropriate term for it brought about notions of immortality and death with its changing skin! Yet it also brought the African myth that while the God-sent chameleon dawdled, the lizard arrived first with the message of death. Was Death simply and really a human mistake?

What lay in store for Bone-rack had truly been determined in that span of time six months earlier.

CHAPTER V

TWO YEARS EARLIER, MCMLXVIII

Graduating from high school in 1968 and being thrown into a tumultuous sea of events was both instructive and prophetic for Bone-rack. Death, transition, and inaptness, it seemed, were everywhere and indeed Death hung like a metaphor for the times. Bobby Kennedy and Martin Luther King, Jr. had been murdered, the My Lai massacre at Son My in Quang Ngai Province extinguished 504 civilian lives at the hands of American troops, and South Vietnamese General Nguyen Ngoc Loan was immortalized in a Eddie Adams' Pulitzer Prize winning photo executing a Viet Cong prisoner by shooting him in the head; the actual video footage was broadcast on the evening news. As if those events were not pervasive enough, the <u>weekly</u> death toll of American servicemen in Vietnam exceeded 500 lost souls.

For some, the American death toll in Vietnam was viewed as the cost of freedom while for others it was contemptuously regarded as the cost of being drafted into the war machine. And although virtually everyone regarded death as a cost, few confronted death itself as anything other than a price tag, and the going rate was about 500 soldiers per week. And so, death was viewed "merely" as the by-product of war or the draft, and not as an independent, disembodied, detached force to be reckoned with physically, emotionally, and spiritually. Indeed, what was that cost?

The emotional controversy of Vietnam was drawn along the lines of "should America be there", "should America leave" and not along the lines of Death as a transition, or as an unknown state, or as an ancient mystery. Rather, Death was a black or white discussion of did one make it out alive or not. Hence, it was no surprise that coming to grips with death, especially as a volunteer or conscripted teenager, would be anything else than utter bewilderment. And with so much death around, it should equally come as no surprise that disillusionment prevailed. In 1968, at age 18, it was certain that Bone-rack knew little, if anything, about death other than it happened. Thanatolgoy, the study of death, may as well have been written in Greek for Bone-rack or any other soldier.

It seemed to Bone-rack that both his country and its way of life were not only changing but dying too. Everything from politics to religion, from patriotism to civil disobedience was in transition. Ironically, MCMLXVIII (1968) was a leap year; both literally and figuratively. Racial conflict raged in many inner cities across the country and the draft lottery was a year away from being implemented – being drafted for military service was a function of birth date in 1968. The country was divided into shirts and skins, into patriots and pacifists, and, for those who did serve in the military, into volunteers and conscripts. The harbinger of change was everywhere.

Incongruity was also everywhere in 1968 as North Vietnam expanded its war effort with the so-called Tet Offensive across South Vietnam while the US ceased its bombing of North Vietnam. Prophetically, the so called antiwar Yippi movement in the US termed the Democratic Presidential Convention in Chicago "the festival of death". And as Russia invaded and took over Czechoslovakia, antiwar Columbia University Students invaded and took over several campus buildings. Not even the Summer Olympic games in Mexico City were spared from controversy as two Black U.S. athletes displayed a Black Power salute during a rendering of the American National Anthem at an awards ceremony.

Bone-rack was very slowly assimilating events and trying to make sense of just where and how he fit in to the larger picture. His family make-up was part of that process. Bone-rack knew his father was a Navy combat veteran of the bloody island hopping campaign in the

South Pacific theatre during World War II. And Bone-rack's community experience was part of that process as well; at least seven of his friends in his small hometown of about thirteen thousand residents had died in Vietnam, the majority of them Marines.

Part of that assimilation process also involved Bone-rack's experiences at school. The very devoted and capable Sisters of St. Joseph who taught at Bone-rack's Catholic high school probed him and his classmates deeply about Vietnam, the nuns being careful to not have a political agenda but rather, be the spiritual, ethical, and moral advisers they truly were. The senior course in something called apologetics often became a lightening rod for "just war" theory, the social teachings of the Catholic Church, and individual responsibility. For all issues, the scrutiny was intense as the teachers and students alike were acutely aware of the weekly death toll in Vietnam, of the draft, and of the political turmoil in the country. And the end game was always the same: pray and have dialogue with your Creator; sage advice which Bone-rack took seriously and practiced.

Bone-rack's father, who had witnessed first hand the invasions of the Gilberts and Solomon Island chains, Tarawa, Iwo Jima, and the rest of the so-called island hopping campaign, spent hours speaking with Bone-rack about what it meant to be a Marine and to be in combat. For an Iowa farmer with an eighth grade education and now a clerk in a grocery store, his wisdom, it seemed to Bone-rack, was priceless. He told Bone-rack not to confuse patriotism with romanticism, that there was nothing glorious or romantic about dying or being maimed in war. But he also told Bone-rack to choose wisely as the worst of all emotions was regret; the regret of an opportunity not taken remained long after the completion of the alternative choice. Perhaps the most important thing he told Bone-rack was that he, and only he, could make choices for his life because in the end he had to live with them and that, as his father, his advice would be always be tempered with wanting to protect his son and not put him in harm's way. At 18, Bone-rack faced a dilemma.

Many of Bone-rack's classmates were intent on going to college and higher education was expensive. No one in Bone-rack's family had ever secured a four year degree. Bone-rack had watched his father and mother work for years to pay off a very modest mortgage. When they offered to re-mortgage the house to provide for his education, Bone-rack knew what his choice would be; the choice was not only easy, it was clear: Bone-rack chose to be what he deemed a patriot. Having already received his induction physical notice, Bone-rack enlisted in the Marine Corps.

The news of more area servicemen killed in action now brought death front and center for Bone-rack. How, he wondered, would he deal with being a Marine, with being in combat? Those were questions Bone-rack faced two years earlier and they were now being answered.

CHAPTER VI

QUESTIONS AND ANSWERS

Others faced questions too, and sometimes answers were delivered like a delinquent bill stamped "past due". LT had questions and so did Sarge. Pig man had answers to unasked questions and Ricky recon had questions to which answers did not appear readily available.

LT's unopened letters from a longtime lover at a New England college could have been stored comfortably with Sarge's unsent letters to an old high school coach; the mail gave rise to old answers long overdue. It would not have mattered if the letters became comingled as the answers were the same. In some ways, Bone-rack's questions were easier because the answers to them resided in the future and could only be answered by what he would do. LT's and Sarge's questions, on the other hand, had answers which dwelled in the past and could only be salvaged by a nocturnal rescue mission to the far reaches of each one's soul. And there really was no more light there than in their first tours to Vietnam.

LT saw his presence in Vietnam through the lens of an ancient Greek warrior imbuing his charges with courage, wisdom, honor, and spiritual insight, anathema to a young woman's love and longing for a "too-good-to-be-true" beau. While he would question why only poorly educated, rural and inner city young men should defend the country's honor, his presumed bride-to-be questioned why he would risk all for a fight no one could win. Truly, this was a fight neither one could win.

Sarge did not see himself present in Vietnam as much as he saw himself where he should be, walking it as he talked it. And a black high school coach who saw so much promise in him athletically failed to understand that coming of age was grounded as much in coming into an age as it was in athletic prowess. The old coach knew that feeling from World War II and knew the promise was a fleeting one, at least he never found the promise! Still, his old youthful feelings and his coaching abilities told him there was no substitute for experience, be it sports or war.

No, there was no substitute for experience and all that skill, knowledge and know-how came with a price, and an obligation. Gaining that experience and leaving meant another would have to start at square zero and make the same mistakes to get to that skill level. Leadership, a very rare quality, compelled one to use hard learned experience to help others. LT and Sarge were leaders.

Both LT and Sarge found the logic to express their inner feelings but they put that rubric in similar places: unopened and unsent letters. Each also realized that most of their fellow warriors would not appreciate the essence of their thoughts but every once in a while someone would come along who seemed not only in need of that insight but desirous of it as well. Bone-rack seemed to fit that mold.

Pig man appeared brash and boorish to those who relied upon first, second, and third impressions. But like a rock in the middle of a stream, he could be counted on for making it across; across the stream, across the tour of duty, and even across life. In a word, Pig man was loyal, some would say a loyal Marine but that was redundant. One could count on Pig man to justify everything with: "It is the 'Nam, man; it is just the 'Nam." And so he had answers. There were very few questions in Pig man's life; loyalty is like that. One of the very few questions in Pig man's life was self-asked: Would he do all that was required of him to be as good a Marine as his father?

If LT owned books with funny titles, Ricky recon had books without covers, without chapters, and without words. Nameless and authorless books comprised Ricky recon's library of lament for God, for fellow Marines, for lost causes, and for his own lost life. If he could just find the titles and the authors he would excel because he had written, lived, breathed, and personified all that they would have written. Sometimes libraries are like that, so much knowledge and authority and so much difficulty in finding the right page, the right chapter, and the right title. But knowing that it is there compels one on in the search of questions and answers.

CHAPTER VII

A GLIMPSE OF TEAM EAGLE

"**D**oes it ever bother you Sarge, that Black America thinks you are a Tom" quipped Ricky recon. "It bothers me that you think they do" Sarge shot back, "but it is what I would expect from a lifer". The tension eased as both Marines laughed. The two had a common bond as NCOs even though there was a huge rank distinction between an NCO and a Staff NCO; they even had different clubs and mess halls to go to. To either, however, the color was emphatically Marine Corps green.

There was a rumor that Sarge once saved Ricky recon's life, but just where was in doubt. Paradoxically, some thought it was in Ricky recon's home town of Macon but no one could put that together, a Black in the South land in the 60's saving a while man's life? But Sarge knew he was a Black man inside a green body, the same green body that every Marine shared. And in that shade of green, just like on an artist's pallet, colors always combined to make other hues – sometimes murky and not so transparent. Ricky recon knew Sarge well and he was aware of the tinge of black and green that was not measured in tone but rather, in character; Sarge knew that too – only he also knew that the tone came with attitude and pitch. Sarge's heart cried for the other residents who did not escape that South Chicago neighborhood, for the anguished souls of his brothers who could not see past color, for his fellow Americans who could not see their own colors, literally and figuratively, and for humankind that failed to see a world painted by a Divine hand with many shades and colors. To Sarge, it incongruously seemed as if the world could benefit from an art appreciation course by becoming color blind.

Ricky recon had a story too, only it was embedded - some would say masked - in his patriotism, belief in country, and in his waning belief in a merciful God that came from not seeing His presence in too many hopeless situations. He was not jaded, just in a situational realistic mode, as some shrink once told him. Not much in Ricky recon's life was complicated except his life itself. It appears the same shrink thought Ricky recon was a good couch case but never had the chance to tell him so as he never returned.

Bone-rack was obsessed with his radios and constantly switched out the batteries to ensure they worked and then checked and rechecked the frequencies to be sure they were accurate; a dead battery likely meant dead people and a wrong frequency meant miscommunication. He laughed to himself, "Now that is peculiar" he thought, "a dead battery means dead people and a good battery means dead people." Something waxed poetic and tragic about that at the same time. Pig man saw him laughing to himself and smiled. "It figures you would laugh at yourself, hell, everyone else does!" he said. Bone-rack ignored the comment while he watched Pig man deftly apply lubricating oil to the M60 chamber and barrel. "Funny thing" Bone-rack finally said, "you do all the talking here in the rear and out there in the boonies you want me to do all the talking." "Damn straight" said Pig man as they both became absorbed again in what they were doing. The situation oozed tenseness like super glue squishing out of parts brought together and threatening to form bumps and bubbles on what was a plain surface. But there were no rough edges here, the two had bonded as only Marines in war can. Sarge looked on and then rolled his eyes at Ricky recon. Funny, he thought, how the pieces of the team fit in the rear. Bone-rack was right, they did want him to talk in the bush – to call in protective airstrikes - and with each squirt of oil Pig man injected into the big M60 Sarge's confidence was more fluid. The kids, as he called them, could (hell, had) killed many enemy soldiers and performed their missions admirably; they were good Marines.

LT was acutely aware of Team Eagle's status and its complexion, young warriors coupled with experienced and tried NCOs. He was also intensely cognizant of the ever increasing demands put upon Team Eagle; the missions were hairy, fraught with danger, and were serious business. He knew Sarge and Ricky recon would go to any length to protect Pig man and Bone-rack because of their youth, and he knew he felt the same way - he could not, would not if at all in his power, let their epitaphs read "Killed in action". While many recon Marines thought themselves larger than life precisely because of their mission (and rightly so), he noted Bone-rack's humility, those piercing blue eyes which stood out from his deeply tanned face, and the contrast between his teenage immaturity at times and his nimble, skillful, almost adroit ability to do what Marines do: fight wars. Strangely, LT never thought about the "kids" saving the team. After all, they were young, inexperienced Marines but they would learn fast and adapt.

Team Eagle was truly a force to be reckoned with by any enemy! But as LT also knew, warriors, even great warriors, died in war. For war, it seemed, was larger than life - at times an immovable force. LT repeated that thought in his head: "Warriors, even great warriors, died in war" and in that knowledge was a self-awareness prophetically gleaned and a glimpse of Reconnaissance Team Eagle revealed to LT.

CHAPTER VIII

TRAP TEAM AT WORK

The helicopter screamed low, just over the tree tops, in the early morning twilight. Another pilot, an A4 jockey this time, was down but it was a Marine pilot. It was not supposed to matter but somehow it did; the "green machine", as the Corps was sometimes referred to, was like that. The insertion bird tilted up sharply and then sank toward the ground as equipment and team members jumped and landed into the tall vegetation and into their fate. Then the helicopter was gone. LT, Bone-rack, and Sarge went one way while Ricky recon, Pig man and a new automatic rifleman, a Marine just in country, went the opposite way about 30 "klicks", or kilometers just north of the DMZ, Team Eagle was now in cowboy country. And no one knew how many, if anyone, saw or heard them being inserted. Although separating decreased the team's direct fire power, it allowed the team to flank in the event of an immediate confrontation and to simultaneously repel a frontal attack. No one talked and every Marine's weapon was at the ready. Fear plumbed the depths of each man's psyche, yet only confidence and determination exuded from each man's face. This was the business of war and they were Marine Recon.

The team trekked on a parallel course for most of the morning until they neared the expected crash area from about a "klick" out. Somewhere, if they were lucky, was the downed pilot. He had activated his beacon and his wingman confirmed movement afterwards - he was at least alive when he went in and hopefully he was still alive.

Pig man spotted the downed pilot first. He was crouched low in thick vegetation and holding a pistol in one hand and a radio, a small PRC90 handheld radio with locator frequency, in the other hand; the pilot had picked a good "harbor site" for the night: anyone approaching the site would make noise and alert him to danger. Ricky recon keyed the small transmitter he carried so the pilot knew someone friendly was close by and the pilot keyed back to indicate that, to his knowledge, it was safe to approach him. Pig man set up a line of sight for protective fire and the new Marine scoured the bush for any signs of movement. From the other direction, Bone-rack quietly and precisely confirmed their location and requested a standby fire mission from air naval gunfire liaison company, in military terms, ANGLICO. He also confirmed an extraction in progress so that birds would be on the scene as quickly as possible. The team now quickly sought extraction; this was always an anxious and dangerous time.

It was Pig man who first spotted the bamboo covered grass mat rise from the jungle floor to reveal three figures. As the others neared the pilot, a deafening roar screamed out. It was the M-60 shredding the three figures, stitching 7.62mm rounds across their heads and shoulders. The nearby tree line erupted in flashes as all the team members gathered to form a skirmish line and pour deadly lead into the bush. Squeezing the mike, Bone-rack declared "Tango this is Eagle, fire mission, I have enemy troops in the open" and followed with pre-established coordinates. From out of nowhere, the unmistakable whistle of the first rounds appeared as Bone-rack calmly but firmly adjusted distance, walked the rounds into the heart of the enemy, and then ordered "fire for effect". The shells rained down and the team could see body parts fly in the air. As the NVA tried to escape the deadly fire, they ran towards the team, their only "safe" direction, only to have Pig man slowly decimate their ranks with short, consistent, and accurate bursts, the hallmark of an expert machine gunner. From seemingly out of nowhere, fast-movers (fixed-wing jets) appeared wing abreast and stacked themselves in a continuous run on the tree line and hillside behind it. The napalm hit and swirled viciously from the wake turbulence of the low flying jets. The screams were audible even above the noise. Bone-rack saw two NVA on fire and engulfed in flames. In compassion he shot them both and then said "Forgive me Jesus". Then the team and their package moved swiftly away until the large, Sea Stallion helicopter, flanked by two gunships, slid quickly across the ground with a long rope ladder hanging from the bird's belly. The team and their package latched onto the rope ladder net and were lifted safely up, up, and away over the jungle canopy for the extraction. The unmistakable smell of the napalm filled Bone-rack's senses. He looked down on the dismembered and burning bodies, and, closing his eyes high above the ground, thought about death. Death received was worse, he thought, than death delivered but he knew that either beat you! He quietly thanked God for this deliverance and asked forgiveness. From the height above ground Bone-rack felt he should be closer to God but it did not feel that way. He wondered if God saw what he saw on the ground.

An instant later the jets were at altitude once again and the familiar thuds from the offshore ANGLICO battery pounded the ground. Team Eagle, with package in hand, was lowered to the ground in a safe area and then entered the cargo ramp of the helicopter. Once aboard, they were whisked off to the safety of Da Nang and their hooches, another mission accomplished. Since they had to return the package to First Maine Air Wing, they got to go to Da Nang and Recon head-quarters at Camp Reasoner - not An Hoa; a real treat. Pig man's eyes met Bone-rack's; how many had they killed this time? Neither spoke; neither had to nor wanted to. But Bone-rack felt closer to Pig man because he was hurting too.

LT looked at Bone-rack intently until their eyes met. LT saw ability and faith in those young, blue eyes but he also saw judgment and sadness; a rare quality for such a young person. Bone-rack then looked down and thought again of how many he had just killed. He found no answers, just more death. LT knew Bone-rack had just saved all their lives but that he also had taken on a burden that he would not soon, if ever, put down. How he wished he could save the young man from the power of death; dying was one thing, being dead while still alive was quite another thing but such was the business of a TRAP team at work.

CHAPTER IX

DEATH IN THE REAR

"Do you want some pizza?" the new Marine asked Pig man and Bone-rack. "We'll buy, you fly" said the two, almost in unison. Handing him some MPC, both returned to their chores of checking the PRC25 radio and re-assembling the M-60. The young Marine left for the PX. It was about an hour later when they realized they were hungry and had not received their pizza yet. "May as well go get it ourselves" Pig man said, "The fucking puke took off with our bucks and is either getting laid or drinking". As they were getting ready to leave the hooch they were met by Sarge. "He's dead" Sarge said matter-of-factly and sat down on the footlocker. Pig man and Bone-rack looked incredulously at one another. "Where, how, when?" they asked almost simultaneously. "A sentry thought he saw something and opened up" Sarge responded; "He got two of the VC, but they had already knifed him and were standing over his body".

LT came in with Ricky recon and confirmed the news. "It is just not fucking possible" said Bone-rack, "How could this happen?" "It's the 'Nam man" said Pig man, "it happens." Sarge thought about the young Marine; he should not have left him alone, even in the rear. Pig man glared at the young Marine's bunk and realized he did not even know his full name, only that he was from somewhere in New York. Bone-rack stared at the floor, momentarily "happy" now he had "wasted" so many enemy that day and then profoundly sad that death was winning this war, on all sides. Angry, sad, incensed and then apprehensive, Bone-rack just wanted to go home: Home to where he had never voted, home to where he had only had a legal drink in his native state of New York but not elsewhere in states where the drinking age was 21, and home to where he had not even gotten laid. "God", he thought, "what kind of hell was this? And who wants to win hearts and minds?" Bone-rack neither understood nor cared why they were in Vietnam, nor did he see any purpose in being there other than protecting his fellow Marines or perhaps saving a pilot. Why did they fight in the south when the enemy was in the north?

Somewhere deep in his Catholic upbringing though Bone-rack permitted the notion that this was a just war, it had to be or he was surely going to a hell worse than he was in. The Marine in Bone-rack wanted to rip out the heart and put a round through the mind of the enemy, but just who was the enemy? Then, upon reflection, he thought "Who am I to decide who the enemy is?" He also remembered that he volunteered for this, feeling it was his duty- duty, just war, hearts and minds, things that were confusing. What was crystal clear to Bone-rack was that another Marine was dead and it was not as a result of the front lines, the enemy, yes – but not on the front lines. "Hell" Bone-rack thought, "There were no lines, no rules, and no boundaries, there was only the absence of reason." It did not seem sufficient to justify the loss of a good Marine.

LT watched Bone-rack from a distance and saw the turmoil, but he also saw the goodness in his honest, doubtful expression. He did not want death to defeat Bone-rack or claim him as its own. Death could do much more than kill the body, it could kill the mind and the heart and it could kill the soul. And Bone-rack, he knew, had a lot of soul.

Bone-rack continued to dwell on the notion he "volunteered" for this, he knew full well why he "volunteered" and that was catching up with him too: An Hoa's memory was very much alive. In the meantime, LT would make it a priority to find down time for his men. But where could one go that death did not follow? To be sure, there was death in the rear.

CHAPTER X

REST AND RECUPERATION; LIES AND MURDER

R &R came in different flavors: rest and recuperation "in-country" as in a weekend at China Beach on the sand and in the surf or rest and recuperation in short hops to Thailand, Taiwan, Singapore, Hong Kong or even Hawaii. Bone-rack's favorite was Hong Kong, Pig man's favorite was Taipei, Taiwan, LT's favorite was Hawaii, and Sarge's was Thailand. There was always Sydney, Australia but that was generally limited to a free 30 day stay for extending one's tour in the 'Nam for six months; Bone-rack did that once and so did LT.

China Beach had the best of Vietnam, a long, white sandy beach on the South China Sea and steaks cooking on the grill. Near Da Nang, it was "in the rear" and a warm, sunny, and relaxing place to be; hell, some troops even had surf boards. And death, it had a place as well, a body bag!

The fight started out routinely enough: one group wanted to listen to soul music and the other group wanted to hear country/western music, Marvin Gaye or Johnny Cash. The MPs arrived, took in both sides of the story and left with two of the soul brothers in handcuffs; it did not get more arbitrary than that. It was about 3:30 am when Pig man heard the explosion. Instinctively rolling out of his bunk and onto the floor, he grabbed his .45 on the way down. The subsequent silence was deafening and then the sound of voices and people running. Little by little, Pig man pieced the story together. It seems someone had thrown a grenade into a hooch where some MPs lived, a fragging: two dead and one severely wounded. So much for the rear and another fucking reason Pig man hated this place. He never wanted to listen to Marvin Gaye or Johnny Cash again; they both sang sad songs - dirges for those who dealt with and tried to escape the aura of death.

Meanwhile, Bone-rack was in Hong Kong being pulled around in a rickshaw from one bar to another. The local "B" girls had shapely enough asses: small, petite, firm asses inside of painted on silk pants. When he went back he would brag about how many he did and what it cost him. But, truth told, he did none of them because he was a coward, afraid of catching something, afraid of getting rolled by some cowboy friends of the prostitute, and afraid of…..well, afraid of God's judgment and God's judgment was as real as death. As grunts crudely and inanely said, "Don't fuck with God's judgment or put Him to the test." They knew! Fox holes easily made one a "practicing" Catholic.

Seemingly, such an ethical and moral digression and inquiry would only be conducted by a mature adult, but Bone-rack was only 19! What an irony, he killed people by the dozens and was afraid of God's judgment for getting laid! Only a Catholic believing in a "just war" could rationalize that one - well, one in combat could.

But Bone-rack did rationalize it and returned to the TRAP unit to tell a great tale of how he got laid, blown, and drunk and to regal them with lewd details. Well, he might have been a liar and a killer but he sure as hell did not succumb to lust or fornication; only in the 'Nam as Pig man would say, only in the 'Nam!

What was difficult for Bone-rack to explain was how he had time between bars to purchase a new Nikon underwater camera, some fine china to send stateside, and some electronics, like stereos and speakers, to send home. And if one added up what he spent on all that, how much could the girls have gotten? It all added up to rest and recuperation and lies and murder.

CHAPTER XI

GREEN

Green is not a primary color and rightly so; green is, rather, a mixture of yellow and blue. For Bone-rack, green held many nuances: life and death, the war machine of which he was a part and the symbol of the Ordinary liturgical time of his Catholic religion that he harkened back to during desperation, but these were not "ordinary" times. Not so coincidentally, the color held cultural charisma and significance for just about everything that touched Bone-rack's life: from his initial level of inexperience in a war zone to that which he longed to see in his beloved Finger Lakes region of Upstate New York. But mostly, green was apt for Bone-rack because there was no primary element that defined who he was while in Vietnam.

The periods of wild excitement, bone-chilling fear, and ubiquitous encounters with the Marine Corps' implements of soldiering (always green) clamored for competition with the nuanced properties green occupied in love, death, and religion. Like Al-Khidr, Moses' travelling companion in the Qur'an, green subliminally carried metaphysical answers for Bone-rack; answers to questions he did not know even existed. The blue seas Bone-rack crossed to get to Vietnam colluded with the yellow fog of war to cast a world of green wherein he questioned death, life, the ordinary, the supernatural, and the love and lust of his ever-changing life. Indeed, green was Bone-rack's St. George, a

Christian martyr he never knew, or even heard of, who slew a mythical dragon. Unwittingly yet prophetically, Bone-rack shared a weapon with the good Saint, the Sign of the Cross - and Bone-rack had a dragon to slay too before he could drink from the river of life.

In the down times between missions Bone-rack thought of the green, plump grapes of the Upstate New York vineyards that rose from spindly winter vines just above the shores of the many Finger Lakes and proved, time and again, that life renewed itself. And in contrast to the triple canopy jungle that shielded the sun, but not the heat, of Vietnam, Bone-rack thought of the green foliage of the Upstate New York hills that moved dream like in the cool summer breezes or provided refreshing relief from occasional hazy, hot, and humid spells. There was never certainty in Bone-rack's life about just what aspect of green occupied his existence, but what Bone-rack did know with absolute certainty was the Marine Corps "green machine" that delivered recon Marines swiftly, silently, and deadly into the enemy's areas of operation to wreak havoc and death and to secure the safety of other Marines. And he knew this as well as he knew the colorless reality of Jesus, his savior. Gauguin's green Christ, "Le Christ vert", symbolically portraying powerful individual and private loss, would have come as a surprise to Bone-rack, something he could not then fathom – but one day would.

So, green, the shade of inexperience; green, the promise of new life in the foliage; green, that which the primary colors of life blended into after death; green, the uniform that he wore in the field for his country; and green, a color that could only be made by mixing other colors, other shades, tints, and dyes of the world with other experiences, were all that Bone-rack knew. And so he tried painting himself in a plush green paradise where death did not exist. The only part of the Vietnam experience that was not green for Bone-rack was the red flow of blood, a primary color – for life and for consideration. "Green" Bone-rack thought, and then the green light inside the helicopter glowed readiness to deploy and insert on yet another mission.

CHAPTER XII

RECON AT ITS BEST

The ambush was classic and well executed. The team knew there was movement on the trail behind them ever since they had been inserted. Outrunning the enemy was out of the question and having them in such proximity meant never picking up their package. The team scrambled ahead and quickly came upon a bend in the trail. They lined the ditch to the right of the trail with their Claymore mines and concealed the detonator wires. Pig man, Ricky recon, and Bone-rack took up a position directly opposite the ditch on the left side of the trail. At one end of the trail, the front end, Sarge and another automatic rifleman stood ready just around the bend in the road. In the dense underbrush at the rear of the trail, LT waited with another Marine rifleman, both armed with M79 grenade launchers equipped with high explosive rounds. Shortly, a group of ten uniformed NVA soldiers, on almost a run, swept past LT and, as they rounded the curve, Pig man, Ricky recon, and Bone-rack opened up on them. Some of the inexperienced NVA went for the ditch just as Bone-rack triggered the Claymores and the NVA were shredded instantly. The more experienced and battle savvy NVA tried to attack head on and were simply cut down by Pig man's short, accurate bursts. The remainder of the NVA tried to run or crawl forward on the trail and around the bend, exactly where they were met with a deafening assault from Sarge and the automatic rifleman. It was over in seconds. As one straggler tried to crawl out the back he was hit with a blast of the M79 high explosive rounds and died in place. The team could now relax and no longer worry about being followed. Bone-rack assessed the carnage; at least, he thought to himself, he was not a fornicator. And that was how rationalization worked in the 'Nam - the whole thing was over in just under a minute! "Over" Bone-rack thought, "it would never be over".

The afternoon rain was a torrential downpour and tiny rivulets of blood cratered the dirt trail near the dead NVA turning once vital fluid into war paint. Sadness griped Bone-rack once again until a voice inside said: "Better them than me". Still, he thought, would God really forgive this no matter what the reason? At nineteen, Bone-rack was confident that he had grown up enough to know that he was square with God; after all, this was a "just war" – it had to be because he had done too much to be forgiven if it wasn't. That same thought and rationalization kept returning to Bone-rack and it seemed somehow hollow. His eyes met LT's and, for a second, they were both on the same wavelength; they had done what they needed to do. But LT saw pain and confusion in Bone-rack's eyes and he saw death winning, emasculating Bone-rack's psyche, soul, and mind. Worse, Bone-rack was not buying his own explanation of a "just war".

The team continued on to find the pilots: one dead and one seriously injured. Rather than risk transporting the badly injured pilot, LT and Sarge decided to extract in place, a not-so-wise choice given that they had just wasted ten enemy nearby and told everyone within hearing distance that Americans were present. The distinct reports form the M16s and the M79 grenade launcher were enough to reveal their presence. The missing ten NVA would not go missing for long either. The pilot's condition though, coupled with the thought of carrying the other pilot's body, militated against doing anything else. Calling for an emergency extraction, Bone-rack quickly ran the coordinates just to be sure that air and firepower were ready if need be. The extraction went off without a hitch and 90 minutes later the group was on board the hospital ship in the South China Sea delivering both the dead body and the injured pilot.

As the team was disembarking the helicopter on the flight deck, the onboard radio squawked out "priority extraction, I say again, priority extraction". Bone-rack and Pig man looked at one another and almost simultaneously looked at LT and said "Who?" in unison. It was Team Autumn Harvest and Bone-rack's friend and fellow part-time MARS Radio operator "Captain Cool" was making the call. A priority extraction request sometimes meant the Team was in imminent danger of being overrun or that grave injuries needed to be treated. The helicopter pilot and co-pilot checked their fuel gauges and gave a thumbs up to LT. The NCOs were already loading needed ammunition and ordinance into the belly of the chopper and a Navy corpsman joined them. The blades began their fast rotation as the pilot pulled up on the collective; they were off, skimming over the waves of the South China Sea on a dead run to the beleaguered Team Autumn Harvest and, unknowingly, to their own legacy and destiny.

Bone-rack took two bandoleers of M79 grenade rounds and ran them around his shoulder and body; Pig man took extra M-60 ammo and did the same. As they arrived on scene and looked down from above, the situation was obvious: Autumn Harvest was boxed in and had been flanked by what appeared to be at least a company of NVA. The team had sought higher ground and was on the edge of a ridge. The ground was littered with NVA bodies. Sarge and Ricky recon both shook their heads in disbelief. The only option was to create a diversion and make the NVA think the helicopter was going in for an extraction in the clearing below the ridge, halfway down the hill. The NVA would cleverly hold their fire to entice the helicopter into a trap and then open up at the last minute when there was no means of escape. The large CH53A Sea Stallion helicopter would simply get shot down and more would die.

LT thought fast: if they started the run into the LZ the ground fire would lighten up and, if they were close enough to the ridge line, the Sea Stallion could drop its cargo ramp and literally have the team walk off the ridge and into the hovering chopper. The up slope of the hill would shield the chopper itself from deadly ground fire. It was obvious the Marine pilots were on the same wavelength. LT instructed Pig man to be ready with the M-60. He was locked and loaded and Bone-rack had "tubed" a round into the M79.

The Sea Stallion began a slow descent, as if headed for the clearing down the hill. As expected, the NVA slowed their fire to almost nothing hoping the big bird would come in. Just as the chopper was at tree top level, about a "klick" out from the clearing, it began a violent maneuver out over the ridge and started settling fast to line up with the ridge line. The NVA immediately sensed the tactic and opened up with heavy automatic weapons fire just as the rear cargo ramp was lowered. Pig man could see Team Autumn Harvest scrambling to the top of the ridge and giving up their concealment. As the chopper neared, Bone-rack could see his friend, "Captain Cool", dropping his PRC 25 and heading towards the ridge. And then, to his horror, Bone-rack saw him go down in a burst of small arms fire! "Nooo!" Bone-rack yelled. Realizing the chopper was only a few feet off the ridge, Bone-rack bounded out onto the rear cargo ramp and jumped just as LT yelled for him to stop. Pig man looked at LT and then bolted for the ground as well, where Bone-rack went, Pig man was sure to follow. "Fuck" shouted LT, as both Sarge and Ricky recon opened up to provide as much covering fire as possible. LT saw Bone-rack, laden with his PRC 25 and armed only with the M79 grenade launcher, hit the ground and roll. Right behind him he saw Pig man with the heavy M-60 already dropping the bi-pod and falling into a prone position. In a moment he saw the first rounds flashing out of the barrel. Just as LT was assessing the situation, the Sea Stallion shook violently and started to settle; they had been hit and hit hard. The pilot abruptly pulled away from the ridge and let the bird free fall into the valley below. "No" LT screamed; now his two men were on the ground and they were pulling any means of escape away. "Sorry LT" the pilot said, "we needed to gain altitude or we were going to go in hard." As they sunk to the valley below LT heard Bone-rack's voice crackle across the comm set; in the background he could also hear the savagery of the gun battle. Bone-rack's voice was clear: "Sky cap, this is Eagle, fire mission" LT heard him say. The coordinates and directions were solid and clear and Bone-rack's voice was determined and decisive. When the pilots advised they were deploying "snake and nape" – a deadly combination of ordinance with 250 pound Snakeye bombs and 500 pound napalm canisters – Bone-rack marked the area with smoke to guide the "hot run" in for a devastating strike. The Marine pilots knew the lives of the Recon team hung in the balance and they were determined to help members of a TRAP team who helped them. This was close air support at its best.

From across the valley floor LT saw the fast movers coming in wing abreast and rolling into position. The comm set crackled again with other pilots taking up position and two gunships dropping into position to mark the fast movers' "hits". This was LT's worst nightmare, but as long as he could hear Bone-rack he knew his men were alive.

LT marveled at Bone-rack's control; he was stacking runs, popping smoke, adjusting approaches for the fast movers, and giving sitreps as the smoke cleared. The Sea Stallion pilots determined that they had indeed been hit but that they still had firm control of the chopper; it rose and circled off the valley floor and back to the ridge. What LT, Sarge, and Ricky recon saw as they cleared the hills was pure hell! The NVA had advanced to within meters of the men. At that moment, the fast movers laid down a deadly ordinance run followed by napalm midway down the ridge line. LT could again hear Bone-rack giving adjustments and directing "hot" runs at or near their position. He could hear Bone-rack declare: "Danger, close, expend all remaining on perimeter; I say again, danger, close, expend all remaining on perimeter." The situation was desperate!

The Sea Stallion pilot signaled he was going back in to the hot ridgeline. This time they flew directly to the ridge line from out of the valley, came about 180 degrees in mid air, and again started to settle with the cargo ramp door open to the back of the ridge line. They were taking small arms hits on the fuselage as the Sea Stallion's back wheels were only feet off the ground. Members of Team Autumn Harvest were being loaded on. Many were wounded and bleeding and the corpsman was trying to work on two Marines at the same time. Pig man neared the cargo ramp and then set up his M-60 in a prone position and provided almost continuous firepower, the barrel would not last for long at that rate -it would simply overheat. But Pig man was hitting the enemy hard.

Bone-rack entered the cargo ramp just as the Sea Stallion took several hits. Pig man motioned to where the fire was coming from to Bone-rack. Suddenly, LT could not see Bone-rack any longer. He went to the side of the chopper and watched horrified as Bone-rack dropped his PRC 25, loaded the single shot M-79 and started an assault on what appeared to be a fire team of three NVA only a few meters away. His first high explosive round hit the fire team exactly. LT could see the NVA standing to fire and then he saw Bone-rack rise to fire again at the same time. The second high explosive round hit the two remaining NVA just as they were about to fire and they went down. Bone-rack could see the fast movers approaching for another devastating strike and dropped his M79 and began a dash to the cargo ramp. Just as he and Pig man bounded in, the Sea Stallion dropped over the ridge line for a wild drop in altitude down to the valley below. Both the team and LT's men were now on board and the Sea Stallion headed directly out to the hospital ship.

LT grabbed Bone-rack by the shirt and Pig man by his belt and yelled in a booming voice "Don't you two ever do that to me again, ever!" Sarge intervened and yelled back "They are fucking heroes, LT, it needed to be done or they (pointing at Team Autumn Harvest) were gone motherfuckers." LT's eyes met Bone-racks, "Don't ever fucking do that again. Do you fucking hear me?" LT yelled. "Roger that, LT" was all Bone-rack said as the members of Team Autumn Harvest and Captain Cool gathered around him. Fortunately, the small arms fire hit Captain Cool's radio and not him; it had simply knocked him to the ground and he was not wounded.

LT then reached out and put his arms around Bone-rack and Pig man. "You two are fucking crazy" he shouted, "but you are both real Marines." This time they landed on the hospital ship, unloaded the wounded, and tried to unwind from the harrowing experience. Ricky recon looked at LT and said "If you do not put them in for a medal, I will." LT nodded, both Pig man and Bone-rack had gone above and beyond the call of duty, as did the pilots, as did all the others, but the "kids" had carried the day!

LT could no longer look at either Bone-rack or Pig man as kids. What they had just accomplished approached the zenith of courage. He knew all along they were more than 19, they were Marines. But until today he did not really understand just how close he was to his men. He loved them with a father's love and he loved them with The Father's love and now he understood both dimensions of that love – something stronger than death. He saw death personified, standing there and ready to take his precious men or ready to destroy their psyches by letting them see too much of him. This death was a cruel destroyer of youth, of sanity, and of life. LT had precious cargo and death could and would destroy it if given the chance, but he may have found a way to conquer death. And, he promised himself, the world would one day know of his Marines' bravery.

For his part, Bone-rack was shaken. Incredulously, Bone-rack was not shaken as much by the day's events as he was by depth of LT's admonishment. He had never witnessed LT mad and certainly never mad at him. The episode only underscored how much death, the threat of death, and the impact of death on others and the team permeated every hour of every day. Death seemed to be this rushing tsunami coming at them while masking normalcy on top of the waves and hiding utter sub-surface destruction once it made contact with real objects, an irresistible, unstoppable force that was not apparent until it reached its destination. The force was not unknown to LT, it emasculated his soul. Dying was the fear of it coming, death was what resulted.

LT understood the leap of faith, the quantum leap between death and dying; these were separate places where those who knew neither location understood nothing of the distance between the two. He knew instinctively death could be conquered, but how, how could love do that? How did one bridge the gap, the abyss, the chasm of understanding? Were Dickinson's words: "Because I could not stop for Death; He kindly stopped for me" prophetic? Perhaps, LT thought, he needed less Ivy League education and more Marine Corps common sense! This Death was both a traitor and a wooer of trust! And it truly was to be found and understood in the heart of life, where love normally resided! Yet Death took up residence in violent combat and war, places unknown to most but a sanctuary for Death. It was as confusing as war and hearts were broken in war.

In spite of the hidden danger and in spite of death personified, however, this is what Marines did, what a TRAP team did, and this was the embodiment of "swift, silent and deadly" – the recon creed. This was, in fact, Recon at its best.

CHAPTER XIII

DAY-TO-DAY or
NEVER CHALLENGE WORSE

The nitty-gritty of a TRAP team's activities, however, was more defined by its daily performance of routine operations in the field. And that meant preparing for, executing, and surviving the tasks that constituted reconnaissance. Some of those duties were mundane, yet essential. Simply eating while in the field fell into that category as did simply having the right amount of supplies on hand; simple, yet logistically challenging.

The pièce de résistance of a combat meal in Vietnam was a potable portion of liquid to wash down whatever it was the edible aspect of the meal purported to be. A good harbor site might allow time for a "group meal" but such was a luxury for a TRAP team where constant movement meant achieving one's objective in the least amount of time possible. And constant movement meant invariable tension about what might happen next; tension because Team Eagle's warriors knew that contact with the enemy was what could happen next. And so water and ammunition took center stage and both had to be carried. Having to decide to carry more water as opposed to more ammunition usually meant doing both.

That death was tied to a deficiency in either commodity went without saying. And so, avoiding death was the common denominator.

Concealing the team's presence in patches of razor sharp elephant grass, in human feces lined ditches, in the proximity of man eating tigers or poisonous snakes, or in a swarm of insects simply compounded the team's missions but provided dimension to the team's task.

In the end, carrying one's food and water, ammunition, belongings, medical care, weapons, communication devices, and one's anxiety driven tension level took a toll. The extreme heat and threat of discovery were no small factors. But Bone-rack knew full well the alternative: standing guard duty, being on an all night listening post or being confined to defending a perimeter. Somehow the TRAP team seemed the better of the two choices.

Serving with others under such circumstances brought about an intense scrutiny of one's foibles and what might appear to be a quirk, peculiarity or idiosyncrasy in any other time and place would seem only likely to manifest a passionate response in the bush; or so one might think. In reality, Bone-rack found mutual respect and acceptance. While there was a lot of "ball-busting", being with reconnaissance was like being with family.

Perhaps it was the common denominator of death, or intense Marine Corps pride, or the presence of a common enemy, but a recon team was like nothing else in terms of closeness in the field; so much so, that the foulness of death could appear almost bittersweet by contrast but not quite.

And so Pig man's brashness, Ricky recon's lifer attitude, Sarge's insistence on detail and duty, and even LT's almost too focused leadership coalesced into a brotherhood for Bone-rack. They were fellow Marines, they were comrades-in-arms, they were brothers in a sense, and they were recon. And theirs was not a false bravado but rather, an intimate sharing of a code of conduct that bound them together much as winning teams bask in the camaraderie of conquering their final opponent; a shared instant of oneness.

And they also knew one another's fears, desires, aspirations, trigger points, and off-limits issues. The notion that recon could give in to certain pressures, that recon could give out to nonstop weariness, but that recon would never give up, sustained the team through thick and thin. And it went without saying that no one would ever be left behind, dead or alive.

If capturing that mindset was hard at the time of deployment, it was all but impossible to subsequently recall or explain. Certain adages and phrases almost described it, but not quite. The notion that one would not take a million dollars to endure it all again but would similarly not take a million dollars to say one had not experienced it seemed closest as a measure of sentiment.

Having a contest to count who had more bug bites after a trip to the bush or who walked point the most seemed perfectly normal at the time. In retrospect, the ghoulish contests amounted to a way to assimilate fear, to overcome stress, and to adapt to the reality of life in the bush. And then the rains came!

Late fall brought the monsoons and the word wet was redefined. The rain masked the sounds of the jungle, the wetness made everything slippery, any protective rain gear made life unbearably hot, and visibility with the naked eye was limited at best while visibility through steamed up lenses was like looking out through the steamed up windows of a parked car. The direction of sound was distorted such that one could not tell where gunfire came from. And worse, visibility for air power or helicopter extraction was usually below minimum. The team's reliance upon hand signals was severely obstructed and any thing mechanical was either covered with mud or too slippery to correctly handle. Even radio propagation was off such that one never knew when communication might fail. And then, the precipitation would simply stop and it felt as if one were walking through a sauna. The most apt description of this sopping, dripping, and drenched existence is imagining the use of wet toilet paper to clean up after a bowel movement!

The camouflaged, Marine Corps green jungle utilities the team wore were often caked white with body salt, so much so that it seemed as if trousers could stand with no one inside them. It almost brought humor to the Marine Corps term of endearment for experienced Marines: "salty". To be "salty" one was encrusted with experience.

The number of rounds remaining at the end of a mission was all too often single digits. And not knowing exactly and precisely the team's location was sometimes, although not too often, a fear realized by the group. On one occasion Bone-rack called for an illumination round only to have the canister containing the flare fall directly on the team's location; an event that prompted a chorus of "geeezus ker-ist" to Bone-rack by the whole team; preciseness of location did not get better than that.

By contrast, MARS Marines had an almost idyllic existence with air conditioned buildings, private rooms, access to beaches, a very relaxed military existence, and many other comforts normally unknown in a war zone. There was danger, but certainly nothing substantial when compared to what recon did. Yet the rear had its fear as well. A sudden rocket attack, a dogma driven sapper, or sheer loneliness brought about by speaking with the world every day on the air; so close and yet so far away. The radio waves and voices from home engendered an "almost there" fatigue; the kind that sets in on a long trip when children inquire "Are we there yet?"

So idyllic was the setting and the perquisites attached to MARS duty, that guilt would permeate a station's staff when the real grunts came to the rear for a day to call home. While it was an honor to accommodate the troops' needs, the inevitable comparison set in; a self-reflection of "could I really do what they do for 13 months?" And so MARS Marines asked themselves the rhetorical questions: "could I really survive as a grunt", "am I really THAT kind of Marine", and "what a sorry sight I must present to these real warriors." Hearing grunts talk about their short timer status to loved ones during a phone patch was also reflective; many MARS personnel realized that their Vietnam experience paled in comparison to those in the field. That said, however, all it took was a rocket attack, a sapper penetration of the immediate area, or a hijacked ride out to China Beach to drive home the fact that death spared no venue. And things could always, always be worse no matter where one was stationed.

Having down time, being lonely and feeling so close to home via daily phone patches to loved ones, and generally being in the rear had a downside: some drank, some smoked pot, some focused their attention on home instead of on the needs of their job, and some became restless with the daily routine. Yet through it all, MARS personnel did their jobs and the phone patches continued.

In the end, everyone who was "in-country" had to plumb the depth of their being to come to terms with the fleeting nature of life in warzone, for death was there. And more often than not, the off-limits, taboo subject was knowledge about the "world" and just how far away it was, yet oh so close. In the day-to-day here and now, home was an oasis of hope too precious to be talked about; it was better to "never challenge worse".

CHAPTER XIV

MEANWHILE, BACK AT HOME

A s deadly and as bitter as combat was in Vietnam, the streets of Anytown, USA were no safe harbors. College campuses, inner cities, and even family homes became battlegrounds for contentious, and sometimes deadly, differences of opinion. And Death knew no venue limitation; death's boundaries were coterminous with wherever life existed and its ambushes were classic and well executed too. Any meaningful restraint of the death ethos would not be accomplished simply by ending one's tour and coming home to the "world". Death did not have to follow one home; it was already there as well. Being "in the rear" at home could deliver the same death just as pointedly as in Vietnam – as college students were poised to find out.

Whether by reading "Stars and Stripes", a military version of the daily newspaper, speaking with new troops just in from the "world", or by direct contact with home via letters, tapes, or phone patches, no sanitization of events could insulate the troops from knowing that the homeland consisted of shirts and skins on the war issue - and people were dying for their beliefs.

And while the country was still reeling from the tumultuous 1968 murders of Bobby Kennedy, an antiwar Presidential candidate, and a peace petitioning Martin Luther King, Jr., a series of other events were shaking stability to the core: the mythical "Jody", the draft dodging, long haired, peace protester, was supposedly finding carnal knowledge of the troops' main squeezes back at home while the radical "Weatherman" organization lost some of its own in a bomb making factory, student reactions to the US incursion into Cambodia began to manifest protests, riots, and deaths at Kent State together with a country wide student strike at most universities.

The killing of Mexican-American correspondent and Army veteran Reuben Salazar at a National Chicano Moratorium March against the Vietnam War in Los Angeles, California was yet another example of death back in "the world". The My Lai Massacre epic headed for trial with charges against Lt. William Calley while the country reeled again from the U.S. Senate's repeal of the Tonkin Gulf Resolution, the legislative measure at the genesis of U.S. involvement in Vietnam. And any possibility of resolution of the war appeared pointless with the collapse of the Paris Peace talks. As if to underscore the futility of resolution, even the Nobel Peace Prize committee could not find a worthy beneficiary in the wartime theatre but, instead, honored the advent of the green revolution by naming agronomist Dr. Norman Boralaug as recipient of the prize.

Against this backdrop, the warriors of Team Eagle continued to put their lives on the line daily and the MARS operators continued to work on the morale of the troops, both quests seemingly futile ventures but nonetheless carried out with professionalism and efficiency - both downed pilots and downed spirits were rescued.

For Bone-rack, the knowledge that he was no longer going to be a teenager seemed moot; those tender years had met a sordid death during an airstrike he called in the middle of battle. LT's and Sarge's unread and unsent letters found justification in the passage of events back home. Pig man doubled his resolve at loyalty and Ricky recon simply confirmed his sorry outlook on the disintegration of the American Dream.

The passage from naiveté to experience for Bone-rack seemed to be in a wind tunnel, so much so that being deployed with Team Eagle often brought normalcy-comfort from the storm! Logic had been turned on its head. "Swift, Silent, and Deadly" began to symbolize for Bone-rack the nature of his offenses against God's and Nature's Laws instead of the mode of operation for reconnaissance tactics. But all of that went out the window as Bone-rack and Team Eagle were called upon to perform. Perhaps Pig man's answer was correct: It is the 'Nam man, it is the 'Nam.

Accommodation for change issued forth on many fronts, some helping, some not: the lowering of the voting age to 18, the implementation of a draft lottery so that those with earlier birthdates were not unduly prejudiced, administrative hearings for determination of conscientious objector status became more defined with guidelines, and the pursuit of the enemy into nearby Cambodia to eliminate sanctuaries. But the more change happened, the further from home the members of Team Eagle felt, what one was returning to was not what one left.

A poignant piquing of mindset occurred to Bone-rack on the issue of "choice". The very genesis of American choice was garnered at the expense of soldiers' lives in other times. And the Vietnam Vets took the place of others who did not have to go into combat. Where then were the basic tenets of respect, admiration, and homecoming for those who did go, whether by conscription or enlistment? If facing death were not enough, why did returning troops have to face rejection, ridicule, and suspicion? Being justifiably proud of one's commitment, patriotism, and loyalty often was at the expense of not being held in high esteem by those who did not go; it was Hobson's choice! And the punch line was that no antiwar protestor could have hated war more than a combat veteran who heard the whine of bullets overhead or who saw the flash of steel nearby. Death and dying, a noun and a verb, a destination and a mode of conveyance, a result and a reason; such was the enigma that hung like a Gordian Knot to a generation of young men and woman who merely did what they were told by their government. And Alexander the Great was nowhere to be found to impetuously cast the dilemma to the ground. The open wound would linger, fester up, become infected, and eventually poison its own generation, and subsequent generations as well, on the issue of interventionism.

The irony was that even with all that was happening at home - pure anathema to the mindset, spirit, and raison d'être of the war effort, "the world" is where the troops aspired to, where they wanted to return to, where they called home. And while protesters would say "Duh – you never should have left dude." those who served would respond "You just don't get it." It was pure irony, as in paradox, incongruity, mockery, satire, and quirk of fate; yes, it was all of that. And the bottom line was that U.S. presence in Vietnam probably was reduced simply to raison d'État.

At the end of the day Team Eagle was a Marine TRAP unit that saved lives, and MARS was an entity that helped others survive their tour of duty in Vietnam. Meanwhile, back at home, saving lives and helping others survive a tour of duty meant never going in the first place; both notions were coins with two heads.

CHAPTER XV

REACTIONARY FORCE

Calls for TRAP were intermittent but there certainly was no downtime for Team Eagle. The An Hoa combat base also routinely provided emergency reaction forces as needed. These situations were a bit more complex as insertions were into an already hostile or "hot" LZ and the enemy not only knew help was coming but could actually see it come in; a big CH53A Sea Stallion or a twin bladed CH-47 Chinook helicopter making a wide corkscrew arc into an LZ from 6000 feet in the air was quite the bullet magnet. And they were targets of opportunity since they likely carried a whole team or more and shooting them down with all hands on board would be a coup.

These insertions were seldom reconnaissance type six day missions but rather, a bail out of some beleaguered unit or another team. In such cases, Team Eagle packed heavy with munitions such as Claymores, extra M-60 rounds, extra M79 high explosive rounds, and even an extra barrel for the M-60 should it begin to melt down.

Escape, evasion, concealment, and stealth were virtually non-existent for such an occasion; the emphasis was on swift and deadly. Tactics were everything, from knowing when to use directed fire as opposed to full automatic, and when to deploy a flanking movement with such a small force to avoid being cut in two and losing firepower.

Worse, by its very nature of quick response, there was little time for planning; who went where once hopping off the insertion bird was a function of experience and knowledge of tactics.

On one occasion, Bone-rack found himself winding down a MARS Radio phone patch schedule only to be given a few minutes to gather his gear and run to a waiting bird with Pig man and the rest of Team Eagle. Twenty minutes later Team Eagle was on its way into the bush to assist in an extraction of an endangered reconnaissance team.

On another occasion, Team Eagle was summoned to assist a recon team in the wee hours of the morning with an insertion at first light. From the moment Team Eagle jumped off the hovering CH53A Sea Stallion it was engaged in a maelstrom of deadly enemy fire. Bone-rack found himself directing air and artillery support as well as medical evacuation helicopters for the wounded. Pig man went through so many M-60 rounds so quickly that he actually had to change the barrel out. The "popping sound" of the M79 grenades from two team members sounded like a snare drum in a rock band and the smell of napalm filled the air. The noise was deafening. All of the deployed Claymores were detonated and, at one point, LT and Ricky recon actually were in a physical hand to hand fight with three enemy soldiers. Fortunately, it ended well for both LT and Rickey recon and three enemy soldiers were destroyed but only after Sarge intervened to even up the odds. This is what the term "hairy" covered. In the end, air power made the difference and all personnel were safely extracted.

These were the haunting moments for the team members and these were the memories that would linger long after the mission. Death became a function of "when" and not "if" as anyone who could do elementary math knew; it seemed to Bone-rack that it was just a question of time.

But Bone-rack found himself dwelling on everyone's death, every living thing's death, and the power of Death itself. Once, when Ricky recon was walking point, the team heard him open up on full automatic. But then there was silence, no AK-47 echoes, nothing. As Pig man raced to the front ready to fire the M-60 from the standing position, they found Ricky recon sitting on the ground covered in blood, not his but rather, a wild boar's blood less than two feet off the trail. It had simply charged across the path and Ricky recon emptied a whole magazine into it.

After stunned silence, the team began to laugh about Ricky recon's "pig roast". Bone-rack had already reported the contact and had an arty battery standing by for a fire mission! As the tension eased, Bone-rack found himself thinking about the pig, about the enemy they had killed the day before, about the trees and foliage that would be incinerated in the fire mission, and about when they would ultimately be killed.

It occurred to Bone-rack that only the pig, the trees, the grass, and terra firma were innocent, so much for a "just war". And where was his colorless God?

As Bone-rack expressed the notion to LT later that evening it occurred to everyone that ubiquitous death was winning. And while some of the team members jokingly thought Bone-rack was turning into a tree hugger, they only half-laughed because they knew he was right. There was more than enough guilt to go around. But guilt only comes to light after the mortal threat is gone and that was not likely any time soon.

But it was that part of the Lord's Prayer "as we forgive those who trespass against us" that gave Bone-rack pause. He did not even feel he had anyone to forgive so why was that phrase there? Why, indeed. The author of death must have been squealing with delight even louder than the pig that had been summarily executed. In truth, logic had been executed, vitiated by humankind. Sarge looked at Bone-rack intently and complimented him on his insight. "So you do not believe I am crazy" Bone-rack said. "No" replied Sarge, "I think you are righteous". And then Sarge walked away to be alone.

Listening to the exchange, LT saw the cosmic irony and bittersweet karma dripping like molasses on a hot summer day; Bone-rack was apologizing for surviving someone else's agenda, a schema that had been foisted upon Bone-rack and others simply because they were Marines carrying out their country's policies. That anatomy of a tragedy was approaching epic, even biblical, proportions.

CONQUERING THE POWER OF DEATH

In the end, Bone-rack began to realize that death and dying were two different things and he was in line for both and reacting to both. What an appropriate name for a military detail: reactionary force.

CHAPTER XVI

DEATH BY SHAKESPEAREAN TRAGEDY

"What about my call to the world?" LT asked Bone-rack. In the rear, Bone-rack was hooked up with a Military Affiliate Radio System Station, or MARS unit; they ran phone patches back home via Ham or Amateur Radio. A one-way conversation (one person spoke, said "over", and then the other person spoke) was, at times, a bit awkward but hearing a loved one's voice did wonders for morale. "I just called" said Bone-rack and they are waiting for us at the MARS Station. Now, the station was off the compound as the tall 60 – 80 foot towers for their radio antennae made great aiming stakes for the enemy's rockets and mortars. As Bone-rack and LT arrived at the "shack" (as the Hams called their station) they got special treatment while they waited for their turn at a phone call; recon Marines were revered by the Corps and something of a legend and Bone-rack was a ham radio operator back in the world. The MARS team shared their hospitality with the two and allowed Bone-rack to run the phone patch. Soon, LT was speaking with his parents and the events of the past few days seemed to become ancient history as Bone-Rack listened in as he ran the phone patch:

"Son, how are things with your men, Over?" his mom asked,

"Things are well, Mom. My Marines are young but good Marines. Over"

"Well, they can count on you to lead them; they are lucky to have you. Over"

"I feel I am lucky to have them Mom; I have learned a lot from them. Over"

"Your father is proud of you as am I. Being a Marine Officer and a veteran will certainly help you get into law school. Over"

"Well, we will see, Mom. Right now, my duty is to my Marines. There are many here who want calls so I should not take up so much time. I will call you again soon. One of my Marines arranged this for me. Over"

"Bless him! And please be safe. Over"

"I will Mom. God Bless. Over"

"Bye son. Over"

As LT finished his call he heard another MARS operator say "it's raining", code speak for incoming rockets. A tremendous blast jarred the station and the lights went out. The back-up generator kicked in and the lights returned. "Wow, that was close" he heard Bone-rack say. It soon became apparent that a jeep just outside the station took a direct hit; two badly wounded Marines were being treated but it was obvious they were not going to make it. "If that just doesn't beat shit" Bone-rack said, "they came to call home to the 'world' and died for doing so; only in the fucking 'Nam man, only in the 'Nam." As he looked at the blood covered jeep and then sadly up at the sky, LT wryly noted the position of the moon, the stars, and himself on the planet.

One of the nice things about the MARS station though was the lifestyle: the radio equipment needed a temperature controlled environment and hence the station was air conditioned. Since it was off the compound, it also had some amenities like a refrigerator and a shower – a real hot water shower! The rest of the evening was spent with LT and Bone-rack enjoying the station and its services: cold beer, hot showers, and an air conditioned room.

On their way back to the First Marine Division Recon compound, LT asked Bone-rack about his R&R. "I got laid LT and spent my money on woman" Bone-rack replied. LT smiled, knowing that the closest thing to a pussy Bone-rack saw on R&R was maybe a Siamese tabby on the waterfront. He looked across the jeep at Bone-rack with a skeptical, if not compassionate, look on his face. "I know LT" Bone-rack replied, "Someday I am going to grow up". LT wondered just how much more Bone-rack could grow up. "You saved our lives yesterday, you know?" LT managed to say, "And you and Pig man saved Autumn Harvest!" Bone-rack was silent for awhile and softly replied, "Ya but someday I am really gonna become a man and get laid". The irony was not wasted on LT. "God, what are we doing here", LT thought to himself. This was a place where simple math did not work; the difference between 25 and 19 was something more than 6! And it was not numbers, hell, it was not even years- it was light years! And how ironic that light years were a measure of distance while years were a measure of time. Distance and time; so apt, so tragic!

As the jeep made its way back in the early morning hours the two drove through what was known colloquially as "Dog-Patch": ramshackle cardboard houses, dirty streets, and what seemed like a million endless alleys that appeared to lead to oblivion. LT and Bone-rack caught sight of the sunrise over the South China Sea; a million dollar sunrise cast its rays over desolate and impoverished dwellings which, in turn, housed even more desolate and impoverished human beings and stabbed the heart and conscience of any reasonable person. Were the inhabitants of these dwellings the hearts and minds they were looking to save? To some, the sunrise needlessly painted and illuminated that which presumably preferred to live in darkness. To others, the "light of the world" and the darkness of death were incompatible. To LT and Bone-rack it was a moment of hope, lingering, fleeting and then gone.

LT would have been happy to simply save Bone-rack from himself. LT no longer cared about saving himself if doing so was at the expense of his troops. Sure, he did not want to die, who did? But the priority to him was that which had been entrusted to his leadership: the naïveté and the innocence of his young warriors - the heart and soul of Team Eagle. And he knew that despite their experience and proficiency they were novices in the game of life and death; and war, this war, was an overpowering force.

The fine mist sprayed across Bone-rack's face even before he heard the shot. He turned slightly towards where LT sat and saw only tissue, blood, and part of LT's left ear hanging grotesquely off his now hanging head! Other shots rang out as Bone-rack hit the accelerator and plowed through debris and litter in Dog-Patch, even hitting someone and running completely over them with a thud and double bounce. He feverishly pulled up to a large truck with Americans and jumped out. The other soldiers helped him take LT out of the jeep. "What the fuck happened" Bone-rack cried out, "What the fuck happened". "Sniper" said one of the soldiers as he closely examined LT. "Nah, he's had it, man", the soldier said. Bone-rack thought of the insanity: he took LT to the MARS Station so that he could call his parents and tell them he was Okay. And in doing so, LT died! "What kind of perverted, demented God would allow this? How could fate be so twisted? Where, where was God?" Bone-rack searched his brain to comprehend but all that came back was "It's the 'Nam man, it's the 'Nam." Bone-rack drove back to the compound and collapsed in his hooch, no longer worried about seeing 20 – he no longer cared to see 20.

In that instant, in his depression, despair, melancholy, and now morose existence, Bone-rack arrogantly felt God had more to explain and confess to him than he to God! If he thought at all, Bone-rack would have questioned where his God was, but he was no longer thinking. Conscious deliberation brought pain and soul-searing torment; and there was no longer room for rage – it just took too much effort.

In the end, Bone-rack did not turn to the easy fixes of drugs, alcohol, or anger but rather, he internalized it in something that would come to be more popularly known as post traumatic stress disorder. If you knew you had it, you probably did not and if you did not know you had it, you probably did; the diagnosis, it seems, was not as confusing as the ailment. All Bone-rack "knew" was that the pace of horrific events overtook his mind's ability to process acceptance and when he finally realized he knew it, he found he knew much more about himself as well.

The author of death had this in common with Bone-rack's God: where were they that he could confront either or better yet, both? If death prevailed, where was its author to gloat about success and if God's goodness prevailed, where was God to confidently claim credit? And if neither were present then what difference did anything make? Or, abandoning his Judeo-Christian beliefs, would Bone-rack just wait for Charon, the mythological ferryman of the dead, to take LT across the five rivers where Hate, Woe, Forgetfulness, Wailing, and Fire would eek out atonement and transition in the underworld? Neither death nor religion brought answers to Bone-rack, just pain. Bone-rack understood nothing of the dimension of death – just death itself. What mattered, and only what mattered, was LT was gone, not by some character flaw, not by inability but rather, by a seemingly immovable and apparently unstoppable force. There was the reality – the mystery of LT's death buried in some Shakespearean tragedy.

CHAPTER XVII

LIFE GOES ON?

The next few days at Camp Reasoner were odd and dreamlike, almost surreal – except for the fact that the war went on, other teams completed their insertions and extractions, and Team Eagle was being reconstituted as a Trap Team; presumably with a new forward observer officer. But somehow, Bone-rack just did not see how that was going to happen; it would no longer be the same cohesive Team Eagle – at least he could not envision how.

Sarge and Ricky recon said little but clearly conveyed the message to Bone-rack that none of the events were his fault. Pig man put it succinctly, "it is the 'Nam man, it is the 'Nam." And then added for the benefit of his friend "And don't be pissing and moaning about how it happened, you are lucky they did not get you too."

But Bone-rack could not get the sight of LT out of his head. And he wondered why whomever he ran over on the wild ride through Dog-Patch was not on his mind; it was as if it did not happen or as if he simply did not care. Bone-rack wondered why he simply no longer cared; had God deserted him or had he deserted God. When Bone-rack mentioned his feelings to Sarge he got a surprise answer: "This is not your fault or your responsibility to understand." Sarge quietly said, "Do not presume to know what Death and God know." It was the reference to Death as an entity, as a person, as a force that jelled all that Bone-rack experienced up to that time in his soul, and mind, and heart, and psyche.

Something changed in Bone-rack as when the climate is unseasonably different – a bitter cold day in autumn or a warm sunny day in the depth of winter; it was a calm day in the midst of turmoil, a moment of comprehension in a state of failed logic. Bone-rack started to realize that understanding Death began with understanding life as a continuum, an ongoing process that Death could never defeat because life simply renewed itself - such was the essence of the promise of life. But just when Bone-rack thought he grasped the concept it would become confusing like the return of normal weather from an unseasonable state. It was as if the chorus in a play was telling the audience more than the characters themselves knew but the choragus only hinted at a concept to be grasped and then disappeared in arcane silence. Bone-rack was getting a scintillating, alluring scent, but not the essence of, life's mysteries. He was maturing and growing up, as if that were possible for someone who had been through what Bone-rack had.

Bone-rack ran more phone patches at the MARS station, and then more phone patches. He went to Freedom Hill USO, to the FASU club, and then to China Beach for a day in the sun. He prayed and then cursed and then prayed some more. And then he dwelled on Death, not LT's but Death itself. God had not deserted Bone-rack. And so Bone-rack looked into the heart of life for answers about Death. Death, the transition, the ancient mystery, and the "immovable force" were becoming more apparent to Bone-rack.

"Was this" Bone-rack thought, "how life goes on?"

CHAPTER XVIII

A HYMN TO YARILO

With the additional down time, Bone-rack got to spend time with Captain Cool and the rest of the team. Things seemed to move slowly and they were in the rear; a deadly combination by anyone's account. Bone-rack had found a way to keep busy and the MARS Stations at Da Nang – both at Division and at Air Wing – could always use more manpower temporarily. Besides, even if it was the rear, standing guard duty was not something Bone-rack was going to do if there was any way to avoid it.

Running phone patches was always a fallback position for Bone-rack; Ham Radio was his hobby. Captain Cool and Bone-rack alternated running traffic (as they called phone patch schedules) to state side Marine Corps bases at Twenty-nine Palms, California and Barstow, California on the West Coast, and at Headquarters, Marine Corps in Arlington, Virginia on the East Coast. Spending literally hours listening to the phone patches and communicating with the state side MARS operators proved relaxing and informative; time passed more quickly and the reality of actually surviving and returning home began to settle in. But in the back of Bone-rack's mind was the reality that he would be returning to the boonies "shortly", and Bone-rack knew all about "shortly" in military terms. Hell, it could be never or tomorrow. So, Bone-rack lived at Camp Reasoner and volunteered at MARS, at least for the meantime until a new TRAP team could be put together. In the interim, other TRAP teams performed the rescue missions.

The phone patch stories were the same: "I am short and will be home soon.", "I am ok so please do not worry about me.", "Please take care of yourself, we love you.", and even "We can get married when I get home." Hope, planning, and expectation seemed to mock reality; even ignore it. Dying dealt with hopelessness, death was the end game. Still, Bone-rack found a profound sense of satisfaction in seeing the faces of weary grunts light up with the sound of familiar voices. But, it always drew him back to reality, back to LT's absence, and back to the hopelessness of "if" and "when" someone returned to the "world". The more Bone-rack answered those questions, the less innocent he became.

For 19 year old Bone-rack it seemed that greater forces were at large which controlled his destiny and that his fellow Marines were more like mythological characters already destined to those forces' designs. Put another way, the deaths simply made no sense, there was no rhyme or reason apparent - and no amount of prevention, it seemed, could overcome or prevent what lay in store. A feeling of powerlessness was accentuated in the rear as if not being in control of a firefight simply meant that events would be beyond one's control to respond or even defend oneself.

Death, Bone-rack learned, was far more than body counts, the loss of friends, or the attendant bitterness of forever saying goodbye to loved ones. Rather, Death was about dimension and faith and belief in life were the only vehicles for measuring Death's weight, aspect, and facet. The less one understood or comprehended life the greater Death's curtain diminished the light. But the more one understood the renewal of life, the less one had to fear of Death's province.

Bone-rack did not have the capacity to fully understand fate or the timeless tension created between opposing forces of nature. Oh, he understood being pulled about and apart like Gumby but nothing in his background would have helped him comprehend or grasp his position as a cog in the wheel of life. Yet in the spring of his life, Bone-rack had witnessed enough death for a lifetime and the light of his world, his God, could only be revealed and understood by human emotions which grasped for truth from the desperation of dying. To know and to comprehend was, in effect, to be undone by that which youth was not equipped to handle.

Much like the Russian Korsakov's mythical Snow Maiden, the light of the world (for her the sun, for Bone-rack the truth) brought a death of attrition, melting for the Snow Maiden and loss of innocence for Bone-rack. And just as the Snow Maiden died in the sun professing her love for Mizgir so too was Bone-rack's psyche dying for professing its understanding of LT's demise; the more he understood, the more his innocence died. Would both Bone-rack's and the Snow Maiden's final hymn be to Yarilo, the god of light?

CHAPTER XIX

WHISPERS

In Vietnam, whispers were the musings of a conscience drowning in a sea of non sequiturs. As the seemingly endless "short-timer" calendar blended Bone-rack's remaining minutes into hours and night into day, empty spaces spoke eloquently of what "ought to be" and not of "what is". Those noisy helicopter rides after extractions, those ear-piercing jets at tree top level laying down flesh burning ordinance, and those terrified screams of mortals being ripped from the essence of humanity; oddly uttered syllables couched in murmurs and undertones, utterances of desperation and weighty reflection. Strange indeed was it that such noisy chaos was reduced to calm and beguiling whispers. But then the musings went from ruminations, to reflection, to meditation, to self-absorbed brooding. Those empty spaces between missions shouted silence in nothing more than a whisper; hints buried in garbled and convoluted murmurings. And the hints were dark and ominous.

In the seconds, minutes, hours, days, weeks, and months of the tour of duty, Bone-rack found an increasing number of whispers: the sigh of exhaustion, the rumor of death on the next insertion, the hopelessness of survival, and the ever recurring lie of actually returning home. Were they reduced to whispers more so by the booming voice of war or by Whitman's fantasized "Soul passing over" into the next world? If a contemplative Whitman's "Whispers of Heavenly Death" did not reveal the secret then surely Bone-rack had no clue. Bone-rack only knew soul searching confusion.

But Bone-rack was not clueless to the illogical notion of war. He embraced it, defined it, and simultaneously rejected it except as a means of survival. Still, the whispers persisted in challenging the day to day decisions that led to death. Some silenced the whispers with drugs and alcohol and some quieted the whispers with desperate prayer. Still others made the whispers into dark humor: "Ye though I shall walk through the Valley of the Shadow of Death, I shall fear no evil because I am the meanest mother-fucker in the Valley" was a favorite; such mindless bravado!

In reflection and meditation Bone-rack sought forgiveness but there was none to be had and no one to seek it from. From God, Bone-rack's conscience told him, but God was missing in action or so it seemed at times. Oftentimes, Bone-rack would seek a safe harbor in a sea of theology only to be dashed upon the rocks of death and upon a veritable graveyard of casualty lists and body counts; many, too many, caused by him. To be truly repentant one presumably professed a turning from one's wrongful ways. But how was that possible when the next day brought more death and destruction, purposely inflicted and with a resolve to do it all again the next day just to survive. The horns of the dilemma skewered Bone-rack's soul. And what maniacal manager of the cosmos would permit such a quandary for a nineteen year old? Alas, even that was a cop-out because God did not invent war, mankind did. Even God would not have such destruction laid at His doorstep!

The generation of yesteryear had aptly described the condition in military parlance as FUBAR; fucked up beyond all recognition, and it truly was. Virgin meat (as inexperienced Marines were sometimes referred to), just in from the world with little or no wartime experience, shot unsuspecting and defenseless farmers to death because of their own fear or died believing those stealthy figures to be only farmers one time too often. Such was the genesis of whispers.

Bone-rack confided his inner musings only once to Ricky recon who listened intently and then, lowering his voice to a whisper in Bone-rack's ear, proclaimed: "Kill them all, let God sort them out." Ricky recon's laughter at the end was bittersweet; he did not really mean that, but he really did mean that! Bone-rack never asked again, preferring the silence of the whispers to the screams of reality.

Sarge knew Bone-rack's pain yet was unable to broach that space except on rare occasions just as when a parent has to wait for a child to ask for help or risk smothering personal development; in the interim, he could only empathize.

And Pig-man would sit for hours next to Bone-rack in silence listening to and absorbing the same whispers that neither could communicate to the other.

Being alone in the presence of others, sensing silence in the roar of chaos, conjuring answers to unasked questions, praying to a God that seemed removed from the reality of the moment, and wanting all the feelings to make sense are what defined whispers in Vietnam. And all it took to be plucked from the depths of despair was an urgent call, the need of a fellow Marine, or the need to be a grunt. Then instantly, a formidable fighting machine emerged, a professional soldier, an utterly competent ground-pounder who perfectly executed tactics, ably delivered death to an enemy, and most of all prevailed against all odds. And all this at nineteen!

For Bone-rack there was no glory in those whispers and no apprehension of the next world, no oneness with the cosmos, only a profound fear of dying and the need to survive. It was then the whispers merged with shouts and blended into insanity: "Bravo One-Niner this is Eagle; fire mission, danger close, I have troops in the open, fire for effect on previously established coordinates; I say again, fire for effect! Fire, Goddamn it! Fire, NOW". And in the slow motion carnage of bodies consumed in red maelstroms of fire the whispers returned. Surviving this did not make sense, did not compute, and did not seem rational. And the whispers said: "thou shall not kill" while the mind said "I shall survive". And the transition from shouts to whispers gave rise to a nineteen year old adult, a crusty and salty Marine, and a humble mortal who truly knew God existed.

As Bone-rack and Team Eagle crouched in stealthy concealment the enemy unknowingly walked around, over, and near them in the wee hours of the morning. The steady downpour of rain squelched any background noise in the jungle. His jungle utilities soaked, his boots squishing with water around his immersed toes, his body and equipment covered purposely with mud and vegetation, Bone-rack slowly keyed the microphone and quietly spoke the coordinates of a location just meters away. And the artillery fell, and soldiers died, and Team Eagle was extracted, and those were the only soothing whispers Bone-rack would remember until many years later; for Bone-rack had silenced the whispers with survival; such were the essence of whispers.

CHAPTER XX

THE LIGHT AT THE END OF THE TUNNEL IS NOT A TRAIN!

Two of the pilots the TRAP unit had saved came to pay their respects to LT, to the team, and to the recon compound. It was a somber, flat moment that had the same quality as soda pop after the carbonation was gone. Pig man and Bone-rack would normally have been honored to have a Captain and a Major visiting their hooch, they were Lance Corporals – not even NCOs. Sarge remembered the Major well and recalled how LT and Pig man adroitly flanked an NVA platoon and provided cover fire while the team extracted him from certain death. There wasn't much to say and Bone-rack and Pig man said even less. Sarge also remembered the wild-eyed Captain's bewilderment that a 19 year old Bone-rack directed fast-movers into a devastatingly effective "snake-and-nape run" against the pursuing NVA just as he was pulled out by the TRAP team.

The Major asked Sarge if he could have a moment and the two stepped outside. "How old are they?" the Major inquired. "19 going on retirement" Sarge replied. Ricky recon saw where this was going and abruptly stated "Beggin your pardon, Sir, but they ain't 19 other than on their ID cards." "Exactly what I was thinking" the Major replied. "I know they are Marines, and I know they are attached to Division Reconnaissance, and I know they are good men, the best we have.

But, I think they have earned the right to let someone else fight, don't you?" Sarge and Ricky recon nodded in agreement. "They have seen more than they should have, Sir" Sarge matter-of-factly stated. "I have talked with a General at Marine Air Wing and he thinks they should be transferred to Wing in the rear as a token of our appreciation for all they have done." the Major added. "We need to get them off the front lines for their own protection," he continued.

"Pig man, Bone-rack" Sarge called out; "pack your trash, you are both being transferred to Air Wing". Pig man and Bone-rack looked incredulously at one another. "What?" Pig man said. "Are you trying to get us killed?" Bone-rack said. "Sorry Marines, the Air Wing brass thinks they are doing you a favor." Ricky recon said. "Well, fuck them" Bone-rack said. "What the hell do they know? At least in the bush I have a fighting chance, I will die back here." Bone-rack blurted out. "Look" said Sarge, "The Major does not have the juice to make this happen unless our top command pre-approved it. Sounds to me like you are both 'gone motherfuckers'." What Sarge crudely said made sense; recon would never have given up experienced troops to Air Wing unless it was a done deal at the top. The two packed their belongings, what else could they do?

Pig man was "short' meaning he only had two months of his tour left in Vietnam. Bone-rack, however, having already extended his tour, had more time to go before his tour was up, like 5 months before he rotated. The two were talking when someone yelled "officer on deck" and the Major came in. "At ease" the Major said; "it should be me saluting you two. Do you know why I have asked for your transfers?" he said. Pig man was direct: "Yes sir. The Lance Corporal thinks the Major is trying to do us a favor but, honestly Sir, people die back here." The Major grimaced at the words but softly said "Look, Pig man, Bone-rack.... you Marines have done more than your share." "Begging the Major's pardon, Sir" said Bone-rack, "but who will work TRAP if and when we are gone?" "I am sure the Marine Corps will find a way, they already have." the Major said. And with that, it was done; they were on their way to Marine Air Wing "in the rear".

Bone-rack settled in permanently at the Air Wing MARS Station in

Da Nang to run phone patches and Pig man mysteriously got an early rotation billet. Life was considerably easier and the living quarters were very accommodating at First Marine Air Wing. Being there permanently gave Bone-rack more time to be involved in other things.

The concrete block and brick building which housed the First Marine Air Wing MARS station at Da Nang, known by its call-sign N0EFB, provided a separate room for each operator, transportation in the form of a civilian van, air conditioning, a shower, and something unique: access to college classes! The University of Maryland's Far East Division provided classes at the Air Force compound on the other side of the airfield for many introductory courses. Given the number of radio operators (usually 6-8), it was easy to schedule phone patches and still have off-duty time.

Bone-rack settled in, enrolled in classes, and began to think that maybe there would be some normalcy. No longer a teenager and now a Corporal, the mixture of good leadership, camaraderie, and a seemingly normal routine combined to make the tail end of the tour of duty doable, even fun. While the MARS station was not on a formal compound and there was an occasional rocket attack, the level of anxiety was nowhere near what it would have been at Camp Reasoner with recon, but they did get rocketed occasionally and Marines still died, as usual, "in the rear".

Shortly thereafter and less than two months prior to Bone-rack's normal rotation, Air Wing began its withdrawal from Vietnam; Bone-rack was going home early! Bone-rack had survived; the light at the end of the tunnel was not a train.

CHAPTER XXI

CONQUERING THE POWER OF DEATH

The journey home from Vietnam was via commercial airliner from Da Nang to Wake Island in the Pacific and then onto San Francisco, California. From there, travel was to each Marine's home for a 30 day leave. But the journey was often problematic.

For Bone-rack, the greeting at San Francisco was a realization that virtually all East Coast airports were rapidly closing for a winter storm inching its way up the eastern seaboard. Rochester, Syracuse, Buffalo, and New York City were already closed. The last thing he wanted to do was spend the next several days at the San Francisco airport. Upon learning that Boston's Logan Field was still open, he opted for a flight there. He had relatives in Bedford, Massachusetts and at least he would be within driving distance of Upstate New York if all else failed.

The big jetliner touched down very late on a Sunday evening at Logan, just as all activity at the airport seemed to grind to a halt. All the food counters had long since closed in anticipation of the late winter storm and public transportation seemed nowhere available. A call to relatives went unanswered, a realization that a phone call before leaving San Francisco probably would have been prudent, but there just was no time as the Boston flight was departing.

From high above the airfield in the empty airport lounge, Bone-rack spotted the flag draped coffins being unloaded from the jetliner he just disembarked. Hearing the jet-way door open into the lounge, Bone-rack could see the steps leading down to the tarmac. Carrying his canvass sea bag, Bone-rack went down the stairs and out to the bitterly cold baggage area. He had no winter coat, just his uniform. Just as he was approaching the unattended coffins, a Marine color guard appeared. Bone-rack, in uniform, came to attention and saluted the coffins as the color guard deftly went about its work of moving the precious cargo indoors.

Noticing that Bone-rack had a different uniform than the color guard, a heavy accented Bostonian asked him what he was doing. Bone-rack told the worker that he had just arrived back from Vietnam, could find no transportation out to Bedford, and that he came outside to be with his fellow veterans in a gesture of respect. The old worker told him he would be getting off soon and would drive him to Bedford himself. After a brief silence, the worker told him, "My son was killed at Khe Sanh in '68, Semper fi Marine." Death, Bone-rack realized, had beaten him home. The worker, Michael J. Donovan, Jr., would forever rebut the stories Bone-rack would later hear about unpleasant homecomings. He did not doubt they existed but only knew that he found a little kindness when it mattered most.

The trip to Bedford was fairly short and Bone-rack arrived at his aunt's house in the wee hours of the morning. The worker had tears in his eyes as he told Bone-rack how many times he dreamed of driving his son home from Logan. The big Irishman said "God Bless you son" and then drove away. Bone-rack stood in the dark driveway a full five minutes, crying, before ringing the doorbell. Death, fucking death, had just won again. As the lights came on inside his aunt's house, Bone-rack wiped the tears from his eyes. He was "home" but he wondered just how much of him was home. "God bless you Mr. Donovan", Bone-rack said just as the door opened.

The whine of the helicopter blades became louder in the background as the NVA advanced under a hail of automatic weapons fire, small arms, and rocket propelled grenades. Bone-rack could clearly see their faces now as he barked out corrections to ANGLICO. The ordinance found its mark but many NVA were still between the falling rounds and their perimeter. Pig man's M-60 furiously took the enemy down but there were just too many. Bone-rack watched in horror as they swarmed over the concertina wire and made their way to the sandbags and to Pig man and Team Eagle. "Check your fire, check your fire" Bone-rack called out into the mike. "Danger close, drop 100 and fire for effect" Bone-rack said, "We have zips in the wire! Fire now, I say again, fire now!" He knew he was bringing the fire down on top of them all. It was no use, and Bone-rack went instinctively for his grenade launcher; he would either save or die with Pig man and Team Eagle.

Bone-rack watched everything unfold in slow motion. He thought back to his childhood, he saw his friends, his family, and he remembered his Catholic school upbringing. From somewhere in his memory he recalled the Sunday school teaching from Easter Season, the Resurrection of Christ, and the power of the words that to lay down one's life for fellow human beings was the greatest of love; it was, in fact, conquering the power of death. By showing love for his fellow Marines to the extent of dying for them, he was defeating the author of death itself: the devil. He was no longer nineteen or naive.

This is it, Bone-rack thought. He began firing and felt a hand on his shoulder. Going for the K-bar knife strapped upside down to his left shoulder strap with his right hand, he suddenly woke up. "You ok man?" said Bone-rack's uncle, "you were shouting!" Bone-rack's every muscle was on fire as he slowly focused his eyes. "You're home son" said his uncle, "rise and shine!"

The memories crept around the neurons in Bone-rack's brain with stealthy disguise and then slipped into his consciousness as if directed by some malevolent force. They danced around, brought back fond memories of LT and others and then, without warning, pierced the backs of his eyes with sharp needles and poked sharp objects into his inner ears. "If only I could just die from it" Bone-rack prayed, but nightmares are not affected by death - they look forward to it so they can prey on their victims for all eternity. That is why they are called nightmares! Bone-rack was sure the nightmares were delivered by the souls of the many he killed, and now they were killing him. "Where is my God?" Bone-rack wondered aloud and then felt disgust for doubting his faith.

It was not the first time the demons invaded Bone-rack's dreams since he rotated stateside to Headquarters Marine Corps in Arlington, Virginia. Still with a MARS Station, Bone-rack's remaining enlisted time was slowly ticking away. Ricky recon and Sarge were distant memories but still very much with him in his heart. The last he heard Pig man had been on his way home to be discharged, but he always wondered with disappointment why he had not heard from him. In the spit and polish world of Headquarters Marine Corps, Bone-rack's only concerns were not getting written up for a non-regulation hair cut or picking up a speeding ticket with his new MG. There was not a lot to do in DC except see monuments; drinking age was 21 everywhere but there were girls, and lots of them, at the University of Maryland's College Park campus. Enrolling in courses was the thing to do if one wanted to get laid, the education was a bonus. At least some things, even partial immaturity, in Bone-rack's life remained constant.

Every night brought a new round of evening news about how the war was winding down. Bone-rack thought of the pilots and he wished he could be there instead of stateside. If he had to live with the nightmares, he thought, why not live with the reality and at least be able to do some good? At least be able to fight a real enemy and not some wretched dream? But he had found his manhood, at last - a young secretary from the heartland working at the Department of Justice. Every once in a while he caught LT's spirit and smiled, "You were right LT" he thought to himself. But he also knew somewhere in his heart that LT knew more about him, saw more in him, and understood him better than he understood himself. If only he could speak just one more time with LT but he was gone from his life forever, or so he thought.

The days at College Park were trying for Bone-rack. Protestors who knew little if anything about the reality of war tried to tell others about the carnage of Vietnam on a daily basis, but they clearly had an agenda. Bone-rack kept to himself and simply attended class until one day he saw a group trying to burn an American flag. He went over and quickly put out the small flame at the corner of the flag and picked it up. Folding it, he placed it in his backpack as the jeers and taunting started. "You pussy" someone yelled. "How many did you kill, puke" said another. "You jack booted piece of shit" said a girl who looked no older than 15, "you look like a Marine with that stupid fucking haircut". The egg hit Bone-rack's chest and instantly broke, spreading its yoke all over his coat. The crowd laughed as one of them walked up to throw another egg. The next thing Bone-rack knew, an older Black man was pulling him up off the ground. As he looked down he saw the student's face underneath him covered in blood and with an obvious broken nose. Bone-rack started to swing and then kick at the student again but the Black man's familiar voice said "Bone-rack, I can not believe it is you! It's me, Sarge". Campus police were coming and Sarge pulled Bone-rack away and into a building and then into a room. The door shut. "What the fuck are you doing trying to kill worthless civilians", Sarge said laughing. "The worthless piece of shit was trying to burn our flag, Sarge" Bone-rack matter-of-factly said. "Let's get you cleaned up, man" said Sarge. There was a loud knock at the door and two rather large campus police started to come in. "I served with him in Vietnam" Sarge said, "he is one of us, a Recon Marine, and they were trying to burn the flag". Both officers looked at Bone-rack and said "Semper-fi Marine"; they turned and left. "What the hell are you doing here Sarge" asked Bone-rack. "I work for the VA and the University as a counselor, man" Sarge replied. "And you look like you could use some counseling Bone-rack" he said. "You are lucky those two officers are former Marines."

The two went down to Route 1, the long Interstate highway in front of the College Park school, for a drink at one of the local watering holes. "I can not get served; I am not a man yet, not 21; not for a few more months!" said Bone-rack sarcastically. "Trust me" said Sarge, "they will serve us." Looking at the former Marine bartender, Sarge said: "Meet a fellow reconner." The bartender and Bone-rack embraced warmly. "Semper Fi" they all said as they downed a beer, and then another.

The conversation ran like water from a broken faucet on a high pressure line, gushing out words, streams of thought, and rivers of emotion; closely guarded feelings, and unspoken sentiment came out as matter-of-fact comments like the words exchanged between lovers behind closed doors. Then reality intervened; "Holy Shit" said Bone-rack, finally looking at his watch, "I have a phone patch schedule with Da Nang in 45 minutes! Bone-rack had worked his assignment at the

MARS Station at night and used his days to attend classes. The two men jumped in Bone-rack's MG and then worked the traffic down Route 1 and into the District of Columbia and then made their way up Columbia Pike, past the Pentagon, to Headquarters, Marine Corps. Bone-rack flew into the radio station located over the gym just in time to run the phone patches with a sequence operator. One by one, the soldiers pledged their love and safety to friends and family. As Bone-rack listened, he thought how empty those promises were as he thought of LT's final phone call to his parents.

As Bone-rack had done so many, many times before, he listened as a very typical phone-patch unfolded:

"Ma'am, have you ever spoken by radio phone-patch before?" Bone-rack inquired.

"Yes".

"Ok, just to review, you will hear your son speak first and then say 'over'. Then you can speak. When you are done, just say 'over' and then you will hear your son speak. Ok? It is a one way conversation."

"Yes".

"Ok, go ahead Marine".

"Hi Mom; things are good here and I am safe and ok. How are you? Over."

"Oh my God, it is so good to hear your voice again; we miss you so much (crying). Are you sure you are ok? Over."

"Yes Mom, I am fine. There are many of us here for calls and I do not want to take too much time. But I am fine, things are going well. Please give my love to Dad and sis. I only have 90 days left and then I will be home. Over."

"Son, this is Dad; we are so proud of you. Your sister is here and sends her love. Please keep yourself safe. We know we can not talk long, but we want you to know we miss you and pray for you every day. Over."

"Thank you Dad and Mom. I will be fine. I am with a good unit, the best. Ok, have to go – I love you all. Bye. Over."

"Be careful Son. Over."

The short colloquy, six exchanges in all, was not substantively complex but the emotions hidden behind those words were immense indeed; Bone-rack understood more than most the profound impact hearing a loved one's voice could have, especially to those in a war zone. Words were hope and hope was life.

As the conversation ended, Bone-rack spoke briefly with the parents while the sequence operator dialed the next state-side phone call; they thanked him profusely for their brief contact with their son. As Bone-rack continued with the remaining fifty calls, his mind slid back again to that fateful night with LT. The phone patch had been so typical, so tear-jerking and poignant; and it was the last thing they ever heard their son say! It was so touching and so sad to recall. As Bone-rack finished the last call and signed off with Da Nang, he sat motionless for a good five minutes. How many hundreds of phone patches had he run? For Bone-rack, that question ranked right up there with how many had he killed with bullets, airstrikes and artillery - only God knew. And that was problematic too, God KNEW.

Looking at Sarge, Bone-rack suddenly felt an overwhelming sadness and need to cry. He tried to hold it back but Sarge said "I know" and the two sat there weeping like idiots, like children, like two veterans who know what war is, and what death does.

"I wanted to kill that piece of shit today" Bone-rack said, "It was pure rage!" "I know" said Sarge "but no amount of talking or fighting is going to make them or you understand one another, you are on different planets at the moment." While Bone-rack agreed with Sarge, he was also sad that he could not find a way to reach out to those who seemed to hate him and explain that he felt worse than they did over what he had done in the war, but that he also felt proud to have served his country and, most of all, his fellow Marines. It also disturbed him greatly that their ability and right to protest came from soldiers who died many years before. It was a perverse distortion and a profound disrespect, one that Bone-rack could not, would not, accept – not then, not ever.

"Have you heard from Pig man, Ricky recon, or the others, asked Bone-rack. Sarge lowered his head and then looked Bone-rack square in the face. "No!" pleaded Bone-rack, "How?" "Pig man died in Okinawa on his way back to the world; a fight over some girl with a soul brother.

Pig man was shot in the back and died instantly; the soul brother went to the brig for murder - so they both died. And Ricky recon was a suicide, two, maybe three months ago in a California rehabilitation center. He had lost his leg from a rocket, you know, right after you left. He just never adjusted." said Sarge slowly. Suddenly, Bone-rack said: "It is just me and you! We are all that is left!" There was a long silence and Sarge finally said: "I have been going to the VA for quite a while; they say I have cancer, they say it is in remission, but I just do not know man. They think it may be connected to Vietnam but, shit, even if they knew they would not tell me. So, I have my counselor job with the VA and with the University. I fill two quotas for them: I am black and I am a vet." Both men laughed and then Bone-rack said: "You have got to beat this Sarge. I can not do this alone." "Hey" said Sarge, "I am the one who can not do this alone." They both laughed again and the black, the white, and the green became a soothing shade of blended tapestry which showed no lines, only seamless fabric of fate.

There was a stilted silence and then a question. "Do you believe in karma?" asked Bone-rack. I mean, "Do you think we are going to pay…." "Stop!" said Sarge, "We do not have to pay for shit Bone-rack. We did out duty, our DUTY man. We wasted those soldiers before they did us. And we saved our guys on the ground. Ain't no karma here, ain't no owing nothing to no one. We are Marines, hell, we are recon, and we did what recon does: swift, silent, and deadly. That is our motto, and if anyone does not buy that, well then tough shit for them. Who is anyone to judge us, they were not there. God knows why we did it." His voice was shaking and Bone-rack looked at the floor. "I just do not know Sarge" he thoughtfully said and then facetiously added, "I guess those are adult questions and I am not 21 yet. And besides, you are the counselor!" Numbness hung over Bone-rack like the kind that comes from Novocain when the dentist works on your teeth; you can touch the flesh and not feel the pain – but you know the pain is there. It seemed like death was beating him, devouring his sanity – the kind of death that did not kill but would not permit one to live – with an equation that could not be solved. But Bone-rack knew love was part of that equation, part of that solution; he knew!

CONQUERING THE POWER OF DEATH

Everything in Sarge's mind told him Bone-rack was in pain and in trouble emotionally. Weren't they both, Sarge thought, weren't they both! But he also saw that Bone-rack grasped the connection between love and death and that his love was slowly prevailing, slowly liberating him, and slowly but surely conquering the power of death.

CHAPTER XXII

RIGHTEOUS?

Bone-rack was nearing the end of his enlistment when Top, his 1st Sergeant at the MARS Station, said he needed to speak with him. Bone-rack figured it was about talking him into re-enlistment, something that was not going to happen. Bone-rack had seen his fill of fighting and death. But when Bone-rack arrived for the meeting he was surprised to see his commanding officer present. "What is this about, Sir?" Bone-rack asked. "It is about you, son" said the Major, "It is all about you." Bone-rack was confused. "Did I do something wrong, Sir?" Bone-rack replied, thinking inwardly the events at the College Park campus were catching up with him; he probably should not have hit the student.

"No Marine, you did a lot right. It seems that a former officer in Reconnaissance Team Eagle put you in for a personal award, a Silver Star, but then he died. The paperwork sat around in Vietnam and was finally forwarded here. You are a hero, son. And the President reviews the troops at the 8th & I Barracks next Friday night; he is presenting the award to you personally!" The room was silent. Top reached out and slapped Bone-rack on the back, "You are a hero, Marine" he said, "be proud!"

Bone-rack did not feel proud or like a hero. A Silver Star, The President, this was embarrassing and humiliating. It was a mockery. The real heroes were LT and the other Marines who died. "Fucking LT"

Bone-rack thought, "he put me in for a medal?" He had to call Sarge! He had to call his parents! He had to…..sit down and cry.

The award presentation line was long. The Marine Band played and those who were receiving awards marched into position. As the Marines stood at attention at the 8th & I Barracks, The President, then the Commandant of the Marine Corps, then the Battalion Commander, then the Company Commander, and then the Sergeant Major of the Marine Corps walked down the line, turning and facing each Marine and presenting an award. Finally it was his turn and Bone-rack stood with a face like granite looking straight ahead and through the President - just as he had been instructed to do. The award citation was being recited over the parade address system as Bone-rack's mind reflected back upon the events of that day:

The President of the United States takes pleasure in presenting The SILVER STAR MEDAL to…..

As Bone-rack heard his name, he swallowed hard and recalled the men whom he regarded as the real heroes….

For conspicuous gallantry and intrepidity in action while serving with Reconnaissance Team Eagle, 1st Reconnaissance Battalion, 1st Marine Division, in connection with operations against the enemy in the Republic of Vietnam on 7 February 1971.

A seven man reconnaissance team while located on a ridge northwest of the Khe Sanh Combat base was nearly overrun by a sizable North Vietnamese Army force. During the attack, many team members were wounded by a rocket propelled grenade and required emergency extraction by helicopter. Reconnaissance Team Eagle was deployed to the designated landing zone to assist in the evacuation of their fellow Marines. Noticing the extent of his fellow Marines' injuries, then Corporal...

Hearing his name repeated, Bone-rack's attention momentarily came back to the parade ground and then drifted off again as the announcer continued….

…entered the fire swept landing zone to direct the helicopter when it landed on the ridgeline. While assisting wounded Marines aboard the aircraft he determined that the intensity of the enemy fire precluded the aircraft remaining in the landing zone long enough for the extraction to be complete. Undaunted by the danger to his own life, he exited the relative safety of the helicopter to help others board and to provide return fire against the enemy by directing air support. Although the enemy had advanced to within 50 meters of the aircraft under the cover of a hail of automatic weapons fire and grenades, he courageously commenced a one man assault on the enemy position and was responsible for killing two advancing troops. Only after he determined that all team members were safely on board the aircraft did he break off his attack and board the aircraft. His courageous initiative, unselfishness, and unwavering devotion to duty reflected great credit upon him and were in keeping with the highest traditions of the Marine Corps and United States Naval Service.

For a moment, Bone-rack saw them all: LT, Sarge, Ricky recon, and Pig man inside the helicopter and then the silence drew him back.

The President pinned the medal on Bone-rack's dress blue uniform and handed him his Sergeant's stripes. As The President put his hand out, Bone-rack sharply thrust out his hand in a firm handshake; "Thank you Mr. President" he said. "No, thank you Sergeant for your service, you deserve this promotion and this award and our gratefulness." the President replied. As the President was about to turn, Bone-rack spoke out: "the ones who did not come back and who died in the rear, Mr. President, they are the real heroes who deserve this award!" The President stopped, genuinely smiled, and glanced at the Commandant.

"All that bravery and all this humility; where do you find these men General?" the President asked the Commandant. He then turned to Bone-rack, and lowering his voice said: "Did we kick ass, son?" "Yes sir, Mr. President" Bone-rack replied with a firm and sure voice. With that, the President turned and moved on. Bone-rack was now face to face with the Commandant of the Marine Corps. "Thank you Bone-rack" the Commandant said in a low voice, "Semper Fi." Bone-rack was speechless but managed an "oorah, Sir" in a muffled tone. How in the hell did the Commandant of the Marine Corps know his nick name? Bone-rack thought he would never know.

After the ceremony, Sarge looked at the medal and smiled. "I can not believe you spoke to the President" he said. "I can not believe the Commandant knew my nick-name" replied Bone-rack. "Don't you know anything after all this time in the Corps, Sergeant?" said Sarge, "The Commandant is a former grunt, not just some political appointee. And every grunt makes it his business to know a good radioman." Bone-rack sat there thoughtfully and then said: "And I can not believe LT did this. Why me, why not the others, why not you?" asked Bone-rack. "You don't know? You have not figured it out yet?" replied Sarge. "What do you mean?" said Bone-rack. "LT thought your were righteous because you feared God's judgment, because you did your job as a Marine in what you thought was a "just war", because you loved your fellow Marines enough to put yourself in harm's way for them and for the pilots, because he loved you and wanted to protect you, even from your own doubt." said Sarge. Bone-rack began to cry and fell into Sarge's arms sobbing. He was now a Marine Sergeant, a war hero, a Vietnam veteran, and an almost 21 year old adult, and he still knew nothing except everyone around him was dying or dead; it seemed as if death was gaining on him again.

Who did not fear God's judgment? What fool would think mere mortals could, with impunity, controvert nature's law, God's law? Little did Bone-rack know, LT did save him, and his innocence, and most of all, his righteousness!

Righteous! Bone-rack thought he might be many things, but righteous?

CHAPTER XXIII

RESURRECTION

It was the following spring when Bone-rack went to Bethesda Naval Hospital to say goodbye to Sarge. Bone-rack would have been a better name for Sarge at the end of his battle with cancer. But in the interim, they spent a lot of time together, like the brothers they were, engaging in the dialogue of the living and exuding esprit de corps.

The time together helped Bone-rack understand where God was, that God did not make bad things happen – that humans made bad things happen – and that God bore no vengeance for what soldiers did - you know, all those lessons that come on the journey to being a man, to being an adult, and to accepting the human condition. As Homer taught and well knew, it is the journey. Lessons like understanding that bad things happen when one is complacent, when one remains in life's safe areas and not on the cutting edge of existence fighting what is wrong, when one is not on the lookout for things that can kill life and the living, and most of all when one does not care about or heed God's judgment. In the end, the Book of Jonah is not about Nineveh but rather, Jonah and God's mercy.

The rule of engagement with life consists of survival of values, of what is right, and of what ought to be. Getting up and meeting that quest for survival is truly nine/tenths of the battle. Bone-rack got that now. And surprisingly, the demons passed away along with the nightmares, ameliorated by insight and truth. With faith, death could be conquered! Sarge had been more of a minister to Bone-rack than a brother.

Sarge's funeral was well attended. Surprisingly there were militant Blacks from Chicago who claimed Sarge as their brother and showed their deep respect for him – this was no Uncle Tom; there were members of Ricky recon's family who explained how Sarge saved their brother and son in a race riot in Macon, Georgia many years before – Sarge standing his ground and telling an angry black mob that Ricky recon was his brother-in-arms and if they wanted to harm him they had to harm him as well because the color was not black or white but rather, green; there were fellow Marines who told how Sarge was ever the peacemaker who encouraged young Black Marines to see green if they insisted on seeing any color at all; and there was his ageing mother who said Sarge always wanted to be a Baptist Minister but chose the Marine Corps because he thought he could do more by "walking the walk"; and finally, there was his high school coach who firmly believed Sarge had all the makings of a champion athlete and a potential Gold Medalist if he chose to pursue his boxing career! Go figure, Malcolm X, Muhammad Ali, and Martin Luther King would surely have been proud to have known Sarge. Little did they realize he was them, all of them - and he espoused their commitment and passion.

In total, some 1500 came out to pay their respects. Bone-rack was simply amazed. Again, he just did not seem to know anything except that he had lost his best friend and soul mate. As they lowered the flag draped coffin into the ground Bone-rack knew a part of him died as well but that he seemed to have acquired a new life, a new faith, and a new confidence, resurrection was about possibilities and renewal.

Bone-rack also acquired some new missions in his life: to have a family, to make his life "count" as Sarge would say, to complete his education although no one in his family had ever obtained a four year degree, to find a way to honor his God and spread His word, to learn more about Pig man, LT, Ricky recon, and Sarge, and to confront death in all of its manifestations and disguises. Sarge and LT would have accepted no less and Pig man and Ricky recon would have expected no less. And Bone-rack would not disappoint them.

Vietnam was frightening, but these new roles were terrifying to Bone-rack. Facing failure, he decided, brought far more stress; even death, he thought facetiously, was somehow more palatable than failure. So, with trepidation, Bone-rack set out to build a life in death's shadow; to demonstrate there was life after death that vitiated all of death's supposed power and that there was rebirth.

Building that new life, however, accentuated the absence of familiar surroundings; Bone-rack's enlistment obligation was rapidly expiring, he was far away from any recon types, his closest friends and brothers in battle were all gone, and spending time on a college campus meant interacting with those who, quite literally, had no clue about what the military in general or Bone-rack in particular experienced.

The rebirth to civilian veteran would be as awkward for Bone-rack as a newborn horse's first tentative steps whose dance of balance made onlookers gawk and smile and yet be unable to assist. Bone-rack often thought about watching a newborn giraffe in a zoo and seeing its furtive missteps and falls, "God", he thought, "Will I be that conspicuous in returning to civilian life?" He would soon find out.

And he missed Sarge! Sarge, William Jefferson Bankhead, IV to a very select few who knew and the great, great, great, grandson of a slave to even fewer who knew, died in the spring, the season of rebirth and renewal, and was reborn in Bone-rack's psyche to live forever – resurrection!

CHAPTER XXIV

POST MORTEM

In June 1972 Bone-rack was discharged from the active duty Marine Corps to the inactive Marine Corps reserve. He then spent the next few years as a full time college student, those early credits at the University of Maryland paid handsome dividends. In tribute to LT, Bone-rack even made it to an Ivy League law school! In between school breaks and summer recesses, he travelled to visit families: first to Florida to visit Pig man's family who had re-located there from Pennsylvania and then to LT's parents' home. He followed up with Ricky recon's family after meeting them at Sarge's funeral. Last, he visited Sarge's family in Chicago.

There was something about being with the families of those men that whetted Bone-rack's emotional appetite, like smelling the aroma of a favorite old recipe or hearing the first few bars of a dearly held old tune – something that made the soul say "Ahh, yes, that is it!" And as Bone-rack's senses reclaimed their capacity to assimilate sights, sounds, dimensions, and the ability to well, "sense", the emotional, physical, and spiritual losses diminished. Some would call it healing - Bone-rack thought of it as being released from death's grip. He had only known one aspect of his comrades' lives and now Bone-rack was seeing the larger picture of their humanity. That south-side Chicago shithole Sarge crawled out of was, in reality, an incubator that Sarge proudly graduated from and always looked back to as a reminder and as a promise that his life would make a difference, and it surely did! Fraught with racial injustice, utter poverty, and humanity crushing hopelessness, its death grip could not hold Sarge from becoming a shining example of success. And most importantly, Sarge never forgot, nor was embarrassed by, where he came from. When a young Chicago boy asked Bone-rack if he really knew Sarge, really went to war with him, and positively knew this larger-than-life person named Sarge truly existed, Bone-rack knew that his own survival was a testimony, a witnessing of Sarge's goodness. Death was truly being defeated here by Sarge's ongoing memory; Bone-rack saw hope in the eyes of that young man and a future for him.

And when LT's parents tearfully told Bone-rack how deeply appreciative they were that they had the opportunity to talk to him one last time and to know how at peace he was immediately before his untimely end, Bone-rack knew his heart absolved his mind of that terrible memory once and for all. Death was being soundly defeated! More importantly, LT was surely at rest; the Shakespearean tragedy had a catharsis!

When Pig man's brother told Bone-rack that he had several letters which told how they were saved on more than one occasion by this fellow Marine named Bone-rack it became increasingly difficult for Bone-rack to breathe. The young warrior who had heroically saved them with his expert handling of the M-60 never spoke of himself but only of others, something Bone-rack never, ever would have known but for Pig man's death. How ironic and incongruous that Bone-rack would see more dimensions to Pig man's life by virtue of his death! Death was not just losing, it was in fact defeated, obliterated, and rendered powerless! And while there are those who will say that such is a Pyrrhic victory, let the naysayers live with and court death and survive – and then answer. Let them look death in the eye and not blink, but believe in the power of life!

And if any lesson came from knowing the fuller aspects of these Marines' lives it was surly Ricky recon's suicide. His family was seemingly mortally wounded by the loss but basked in the warmth of Bone-rack's admiration for him. As they told it, no one in the family really understood him in life but came to know his demons, and his full dimension, in his death. What death had seemingly destroyed, in reality brought the family out of chaos and closer together, Ricky recon's death was not an ending but rather, a beginning! Death could never, ever prevail where love resides and Ricky recon was truly loved and admired by his family.

And so, an autopsy of the loss of Bone-rack's fellow Marines yielded forensic results: death was not the cause of their demise but rather, the genesis of their memories. If death could not kill, then where was its power? It could only make some brood but it could not extinguish the love that was there nor the memory which remained; such an impotent yet omnipresent force!

But brooding could come and go in an instant for Bone-rack, sometimes precipitated by the most innocuous triggers – a smell, an artifact, a picture, or saying – and just as easily dismissed by a less pensive mood or a prayerful moment.

Bone-rack happened upon a radio event one day, something called a Ham-fest, where ham radio operators went to buy and sell used radio gear. At one table of "military surplus" he spotted a PRC25 radio, a simple artifact, which had obviously seen better days. The vendor asked Bone-rack if he knew what it was. As Bone-rack deftly assembled the battery pack to the unit, turned it on, and adjusted the volume, a small group gathered. "Hey" someone asked "How much does that weigh?" Without hesitation Bone-rack answered "23 pounds, not including the auxiliary antenna." For what seemed like just an instant Bone-rack drifted back: "Check your fire, I say again, check your fire. Drop 100 and fire for effect." Someone interrupted Bone-rack's space with "That's a new handset on the rig, you know." Bone-rack opened his eyes and stared for a moment at the vendor before it registered; he then gave the handset back to the vendor. There was an awkward moment of silence and Bone-rack simply left the table. As he did, he heard the vendor say to another: "Well, it takes all kinds to make a world" followed by laughter.

"Yes", Bone-rack thought to himself, "it did take all kinds to make a world; even war veterans." Bone-rack went home that day and realized how much he missed his brothers on Team Eagle; the pain was excruciating like fingernails pulled off without warning! But, the pain subsided as Bone-rack took hold of his emotions and hugged his children; here, in his arms, was life after death!

On another occasion, Bone-rack was attending Mass; a prayerful moment. It was the Easter liturgical season and the homily dealt with life, death, resurrection, rebirth, and conquering the power of death. An uncanny calm came over Bone-rack and coursed through his veins and arteries like an opiate. The priest's voice suddenly echoed Sarge's and the parishioner seated next to him looked like Pig man! As Bone-rack turned to look around him he thought he saw LT sitting with Ricky recon. As the congregation stood, Bone-rack realized he was already standing! How long had he been standing? Had he stood there through the homily? At the end of Mass, Bone-rack went to thank the priest for the homily and to tell him how meaningful it was. The elderly priest listened politely, intently and then softly said, "Thank you for your service and welcome home son. God Bless." Indeed, Bone-rack was home, with his God, with his family, and with himself.

There were other awkward moments as well, a professional setting with a simple colloquy and a saying which led yet again to a trigger. Bone-rack recalled interviewing for an appointed judge's position. Since the appointment was by the governor and the applicants were from all over New York State, the process was carried out in the Big Apple! The committee had its offices at the World Trade Center on the 57th Floor of Tower Two. The interviewing committee reviewed many aspects of the applicants' backgrounds and the questioning was intense. At one point a committeeperson noted Bone-rack's prior combat experience as a Marine and asked: "One of the things we try to assess is demeanor. In light of your combat experiences, do you feel you have the appropriate sensitivity for a judge's position? You know, sometimes you would have to make stressful, on the spot, decisions!" Bone-rack laughed, inappropriately so to the others in the room, and looked at the faces of the other committee members who quizzically were looking for a response. Bone-rack answered with a question: "Which part of the combat experience would you be referring to, Sir?" he said. Stammering and noticeably off his game, the committee member said: "Well, the stress, the anger, perhaps the abruptness; you know, these things all have an impact on demeanor." Bone-rack politely, but pointedly asked: "Are there any further questions?" The silence was deafening and no committee member looked at him directly.

Bone-rack never got the judicial appointment but he often wondered if the committeeperson asking the question was at the office on September 11, 2001 and was, perhaps, better able to understand his own question upon sober reflection; perhaps not.

As the years progressed, Bone-rack kept in touch with all the families until one by one most passed on. The contact began as physical visits, changed to letters and calls as life got "busy", and then reverted to email for some. Bone-rack attended the funerals of all the family members having only missed one while on a vacation outside of the country. And although Bone-rack tried to find Mr. Donovan in Boston, the search proved elusive.

LT was right, measurement of the abyss lying between those who experienced violent combat and those who had been spared the experience was not calculated in depth but rather, in the distance of light years; "after death" was truly a time and a place where the passage from naiveté to experience contemplated both life and death - a concept unfathomable to the uninitiated and truly post mortem.

CHAPTER XXV

SỰ CHẾT

T he notion of "after death" began to bring a whole array of thoughts
to Bone-rack in his post military doings. Could one learn something
about death from an adversary? Bone-rack thought so. Long after
his departure from Vietnam as a Marine, and during his student
years, Bone-rack thought about the level of death occasioned by the
Vietnamese; after all, it was something he contributed directly and
indirectly to as a grunt and it was often rumored by the Vietnamese
government to be in excess of three million lost souls. And while the
Vietnamese referred to the war for the most part as "The American
War", it was readily apparent that death (sự chết), or the act of someone's
dying, Cái chết, had its own custom, its own notion, and its own belief
structure notwithstanding who was responsible politically. Indeed for
many Vietnamese, traditional customs were rooted in Buddhism or
Confucianism with attendant beliefs in reincarnation and the ongoing
life of the soul. As such, reaping what one sowed while in the human
form had consequences; a sobering thought for Bone-rack.

Those air strikes, "snake and nape" hits, artillery barrages, and
naval gunfire devastations killed hundreds if not more. But it was the
collateral damage - the peasant farmers in An Hoa, the pedestrian in
"Dog-Patch, and countless unknown others simply in the way of the
ordinance - that gave rise to Bone-rack's concern. Although he had

discussed "karma" with Sarge and came to believe that he did what he had to do as a grunt, there was that aspect of doing what he did not have to do that troubled Bone-rack: the type of action which created victims as opposed to military losses. Where were their souls at? And what, in their belief structure, did they come back as in post-life form? And would that come home to roost in Bone-rack's life now or in the hereafter?

A thought permeated Bone-rack's conscience: what was the Vietnamese rationale for such beliefs; was it purely religious or was it something more? Bone-rack was drawn to Vietnamese Americans, especially those who had known the war, be it from the perspective of the Vietnam War or from the perspective of the American War. Time and again, conversations turned to passing on values from one generation to the next and the use of rituals to insure that the decedent's memory and beliefs were passed on to another generation. In many ways, those who fought for a unified Vietnam were viewed by their countrymen as that nation's "greatest generation".

Customs such as bringing a dying family member home to face the transition form life to death among close family members, having a family member (usually the eldest child) record the last thoughts of the dying family member, and limiting what immediate and direct family members could do in the instant aftermath of the loss – such as not marrying or making life changing decisions for an appropriate time - brought focus to the enormity of the loss. And within that focus Bone-rack found a form of closure somewhere between karma and justice.

Death was the enemy and it could be conquered by life imbuing memories, sustaining values, and family structures which promoted the good works of one's life to one's progeny. Hidden within those death rituals were mechanisms to defeat Death's hold much like an oven mitten acted as a buffer to the utensil's heat on the human hand. The similarity in religious thought, be it Christian, Buddhist or otherwise, of seeing past the human loss and gazing onto the indestructibility of the soul seemed to speak volumes to Bone-rack. Here in diverse customs was a common denominator and a common loss and from the human ashes of that destruction, a vehicle to conquer Death - notably found only in life and among the living.

Celebrating the lives of those lost, remembering their cherished memories, carrying on their values, and pointing out the truth of their existences vitiated Death's hold, heavy thoughts for a twenty-one year old combat veteran but de rigueur for the shift from naïveté to experience in the game of life on planet Earth and, probably, in the universe. Neither the Vietnam War nor the American War killed, Death killed, and the distinction was not a subtle one.

Death, sự chết, the difference was not a war but rather, a force and as physics teaches, a force has properties and limits.

CHAPTER XXVI

LIFE?

In the aftermath of Bone-rack's wartime experiences lay life or more poignantly, existence. But existence ran the gamut from reality to survival. Steely-eyed determination sometimes ran amuck in wild mood swings that pitted anger against passion. Foggy minded exuberance oftentimes begat next day remorse at losing sight of the goal. And while those closest to Bone-rack were sometimes pushed away, those remote enough to be considered "safe" were too often embraced. But, in time, reality's owner – Faith- emerged to claim ownership of Bone-rack's soul and of what remained of his life. And slowly, survival morphed into reality and existence became bearable, even embraceable for Bone-rack.

And death, cowered by Faith's strength, realized it had done all it could do to those in Bone-rack's life and relegated itself to a word, to a noun, to a simple fact of existence. And while Bone-rack respected death's presence, he also knew he had taken all that death could deliver and survived. Bone-rack also knew that Faith had delivered him to this realization.

But while those days were faith-filled, they were also a roller coaster of emotion. Mundane, everyday predicaments paled in comparison to an insertion or extraction. Bone-rack's lack of empathy for other's troubles was more than once interpreted as callous disregard. But fellow students, professional acquaintances, work colleagues, and even family did not, could not, compare to the brotherhood of LT, Sarge, Ricky recon, or Pig man. And the only ones who could understand that were dead! Or so Bone-rack thought.

Contact with other veterans came slowly, creeping into Bone-rack's life like remembrances of a long forgotten dream. But one day, at the request of a friend, Bone-rack went to visit a Marine at a nearby Veteran's Administration hospital; a terribly broken Marine who had long since lost his job, his family, and seemingly his mind. Answers to questions came sporadically until Bone-rack asked the Marine his MOS: a reconner who helped save downed pilots in Vietnam a full year before Bone-rack's tour of duty! The anticipated one hour interview spilled over into closing time for visitation, some four hours later. The bond between Bone-rack and the Marine was instantaneous. As Bone-rack rose to leave he mentioned with sincerity and compassion that they had a lot in common; the response would never leave Bone-rack's memory: "We have both been pursued by Death" the Marine said and continued "but how did you manage to defeat him? God has plans for you!" Bone-rack reeled from the observation and suddenly LT, Sarge, Ricky recon and Pig man were larger than life, standing by him and assuring Bone-rack that he did, indeed, defeat death. As he departed the hospital the heavy rain masked Bone-rack's tears. Death, relentless Death; at least he would have an opportunity to help save this Marine – or so Bone-rack thought.

The news of the Marine's suicide obliterated Bone-rack's game face and shook his soul, his faith, his very being. Bone-rack struggled to marshal the positive elements of his existence: his children, his work for justice, and most of all his faith. This was more than survivor's guilt; this was desperation to prove Death wrong, to challenge its life destroying ability. But in those thoughts came Bone-rack's resolve. He would live his life, make it productive, make it count as Sarge did with his, and go toe-to-toe with Death's emasculating dance of demise. Mark, Hippolyta, Craig, Eddie, Shawn, Becky, Crawford, Chester, Bennett, Patrick, Peter, Robert, Chad, and Andrew; all suicides, all friends from every walk of life who chose something other than life! But, why would they do that? It was an enigma ensconced within some unfathomable mystery to Bone-rack; a sad and cruel insult to loved ones left behind who could only hope that their son, daughter, parent, sibling or friend was, at last, at peace. How they could abandon the primordial need to survive by surrendering that which the Almighty gave so freely though was beyond Bone-rack's comprehension, but not beyond his enmity for the dark one. Yet the names of their loved ones, children, and parents and the lives they carried on dwarfed Death's casualty list. With each loss came deeper faith, deeper resolve, and deeper commitment to the pursuit of life and the living by all affected.

And while the loved ones left behind would forever wonder if a word, a gesture, or a moment spent listening could have changed the outcome, Bone-rack knew that such tenacious and desperate thoughts were only in the lexicon of the living; in truth, it was a vain belief rooted in the mistaken notion that one could ever live life for another. Life has to be chosen, wanted, and most of all lived; anything less was an invitation to the dark one. In all fairness to those who so fervently longed for an answer, their ability to carry on with life in the shadow of such loss was an immortal rebuff to the dark one; a stinging defeat to the dark side.

Bone-rack thought back to all the times he and Team Eagle endured oppressive heat, drenching rain, insects, exposure, and most of all fear to preserve not only their own lives but those of the endangered pilots and crew as well. He thought of how much death he and Team Eagle delivered to preserve their own lives. And he thought of his religious belief in a God who delivered his only Son to death so that humankind could live. And there it was: love! Love for another trumped all that death could deliver. And it explained why a world of haters wanted to banish the name of Jesus under the guise of political correctness. Instead of adding their own religious leader to the name of Jesus they would seek to remove any name; and thus was the fallacy of their claimed religion exposed.

All that was left was Bone-rack's soul searching question: life?

EPILOGUE

The ignominious end to the Vietnam Conflict did not surprise or bother Bone-rack; the war was certainly not lost by the veterans, as the enemy could not claim a single, strategic military victory in more than ten years of fighting. Their only lot was to win by political default. Clearly, Marines and all U.S. military gave much, much better to the enemy than they got in terms of casualties. This was a political decision foisted upon a no longer caring American electorate.

Bone-rack was disturbed rather by the gross loss of life and opportunity. The only time he could remember being bothered by post war comments was when one veteran bragged that at least the names of U.S. dead fit on a wall! From Bone-rack's perspective, the number of dead was an utter waste on both sides and there was no reason to bolster death's persona or prowess at destruction of lives. It was fairly obvious to most Vietnam veterans that while the country was at war, America was engaged in a transformative identity crisis; those who served certainly owed no apologies to their country while those who refused to honor the country's veterans had only themselves, and perhaps the future of their county, to live with.

And so Bone-rack simply moved on. Degrees and titles passed along with the years for Bone-rack: college graduate, trial lawyer, husband, father, former Marine, patriot, politician, and, at age 50, a

Master of Divinity Degree recipient. There were restless times and a failed marriage that proudly bore him two sons. And then a subsequent marriage that proudly bore him a son and a beautiful daughter. God truly blessed Bone-rack's life; it assured him he was led by Divine Providence and not some imaginary magnetic compass marking out the bearings over a map of life's options.

At times, Bone-rack wished he could share his children with LT, Sarge, Ricky recon, and Pig man, but there was so much, and so little, to say – so much to explain, and no words to explain it, and no one to explain it to.

Instead, Team Eagle became a locked compartment within Bone-rack's psyche, except when the memories gave rise to passion that needed expression. One such instance was Bone-rack's successful campaign to secure a posthumous Silver Star for Pig man, honoring him for his role in the rescue of Team Autumn Harvest. He watched with admiration as Pig man's family received the award at a November 10th Marine Corps birthday celebration; the real savior of that day, in Bone-rack's opinion, was finally honored. And when the Marine Corps opened its new National Museum of the Marine Corps, Bone-rack secured an engraved brick for each team member to forever honor their place among their colleagues and to praise their honor, courage, and commitment.

But none of Bone-rack's post service life and accomplishments was done alone; Pig man, LT, Sarge, and Ricky recon traveled down many paths with him, guarding the way, taking out the bad guys, providing inspiration, collectively urging him on to success and providing him with judgment - judgment that helped him to be principled, and to fight for what was right with a passion. In times of doubt, they were there to reassure, in times of need, they were there to rely upon, in times of unpopularity, they were "simply" there – he was not alone, and in times of loss, their memories stood solid in Bone-rack's psyche. They were never, ever forgotten and their memory lived on in Bone-rack's deepest recesses where death could not erase their sustenance of Bone-rack's life. And Bone-rack knew that when his time came, they would be there to welcome him home.

Funny how they served on the front lines and died in the rear; it seems we are safest when we are on the front lines. Perhaps it is God's way of telling us we are protected when we are doing our duty and His work on the front lines and that the real danger lies in dropping our guards and becoming complacent in the face of genocide, terrorism, and repression of the human spirit and even in the face of our sometimes mundane existence.

The fallacy in that argument, if there be one, is that others may be destroyed by what we do on life's front lines, so where is their safety? Maybe those are adult questions that only older human beings can answer, like centuries old human beings. Or maybe that is just war or the "human condition". Bone-rack no longer thought that maybe "it's the 'Nam man, it's just the 'Nam" or that, as a child of the universe, he was not old enough to know better. But maybe, just maybe, it is the price humankind pays for conquering the power of death. Unpacking that question is akin to deciphering a Zen riddle, as in someone says death and the correct response is sunrise. Not so curiously, Bone-rack understood that answer to the riddle! And so do God's children.

Over the years and at quiet times, Bone-rack would read the citation for the Silver Star and he would always stop at the words "**for killing two advancing troops**". Who were they, how old were they; Bone-rack would never know just like he would never, ever forget their surprised faces as they burned and died. Faces, Bone-rack would then look at the faded pictures and faces of Pig man, LT, Sarge, and Ricky recon. He never shared his observations and emotions about them with his wife and children.

How does one explain killing to children? How does one say to loved ones: "There is a part of me you could not possibly fathom?" How does one advocate peace, tolerance, justice and forbearance and yet admit that when put to the metal, only survival meant anything? And how does one say to flesh and blood, "Do as I say, not as I have done" and maintain any credibility?

And yet, how does one teach that some things such as ethnic

cleansing, crimes against humanity, terrorism, and hate must be opposed with what ever means necessary?

No, somehow they just would not understand; not that they would not have tried or cared to understand, but just because there are things about war incapable of being shared, beyond words, and found only in some "Twilight Zone" space located somewhere in one's middle age, right after puberty and just before senility - somewhere between life's promise and death's shadow.

Now in his sixties, Bone-rack recalled his father's advice. Notwithstanding all that he had been through, he had no regrets, perhaps some misgivings on the loss of life, but no regrets – he had chosen wisely.

Bone-rack now looked back and remembered how Ricky recon thought that if they had been discovered in the jungle that night, Team Eagle still would have killed more than four hundred enemy soldiers who unknowingly walked literally over the top of their enemy with their boots and sandals. With all due respect to Sarge, Bone-rack now thought that Ricky recon was absolutely and sadly, even tragically, right; let no one believe that in that time and in that place the warrior Marines of Reconnaissance Team Eagle could not have prevailed and accomplished their mission, even if grotesquely out numbered. And the notion was not one born of arrogance or ego or smugness. The notion revealed a poignant conundrum for Bone-rack: heart pumping pride and supreme confidence in Team Eagle was coupled with heartrending humility about the destruction of so many of God's children. And those memories were tempered with the knowledge of how much good MARS personnel did for so many with their phone patches, how much comfort the voice of a loved one meant when so far away. The notion brought poise and equilibrium to Bone-rack.

For Bone-rack it was ironic, yet soothing, that the same voice which called in the naval gunfire, airstrikes and artillery also enabled the phone patches. Perhaps there was balance in that and perhaps more: that humans are capable of both good and bad and in the end must choose between right and wrong, between good and bad; the essence of choice lays within the mind and affects the soul and for every time there is truly a biblical season -such is the quintessence of humanity and such is the promise of life.

And self-consciously, humiliatingly, and embarrassingly, Bone-rack also looked back and remembered An Hoa and three civilian farmers; a peasant family, whose only "mistake" was to be on the same planet, in the same location, and at the same time two governments disagreed with one another. As innocent as the air occupying that space and that time, their fate and Bone-rack's were inextricably intertwined in a milieu known as the fog of war. But for Bone-rack there never was, or ever would be, any fog, only gross inexperience and unforgiveable incompetence. Others could argue, rationalize, and justify but as Bone-rack sadly and prophetically knew, others did not pull the trigger, not once, not twice, but three times. And while he would take that to his grave, Bone-rack knew that only by embracing the truth (and telling the truth) of their deaths could he honor their lives. If death could attach any lingering strings to Bone-rack's heart, it was these senseless deaths that could either torment the rest of his days or serve as an opportunity for him to bear witness to the truth, and in that opportunity, in that quest, was "conquering the power of death" conceived, pursued, and nurtured. And isn't that what humankind is called to do: bear witness to the truth?

* * * * *

The Memorial Day parade passed by and there was a spine tingling flyover by Navy jets. The crowd sitting on the ground was awed by the stomach vibrating sound of the low flying aircraft in perfect formation. Bone-rack stood up for the Marine color guard marching by in perfect lockstep, looking smart and proud. He removed his USMC hat and placed it over his heart as the colors passed by and as the jet engines whine slowly drifted away. He noticed the crowd was still sitting. For a moment he heard the radio crackle in his head with a blurred combination of "I say again, check your fire, check your fire" and "this is a one way communication Ma'am, and your son will speak first and say over". He drifted back to a very young voice saying: "Are those Marines?" Bone-rack looked down at a young girl with very blue eyes looking up at him.

117

"Yes, they are Marines, our country's finest" Bone-rack said. And then he drifted off in thought as the color guard continued on their way. He thought of Mr. Donovan's sadness and he wept.

Bone-rack humbly bowed his head and quietly said: "Thank you Lord, and I am sorry for what I have done to Your other children; I am just a child, Your child, and Your Will be done." Perhaps it was the wind, perhaps Bone-rack's imagination, but he thought he heard a chorus; a murmuring of "Amen" from LT, Sarge, Pig man, and Ricky recon. He heard his own father's voice say: "Well done, son." And then the moment was gone.

Bone-rack looked around and saw the crowd still sitting while he was standing. In the distance he saw someone else standing but he could not make out the person's face. He had seen the person many times before and he knew who it was, always near yet never distinguishable. Bone-rack knew he would meet that person some day. But he would meet that person on his own terms and that person would respect Bone-rack and Bone-rack's God. Bone-rack looked back and the person was gone. Bone-rack smiled wryly, Death had a lot more to explain to him than he to Death; for as St. Paul boldly and prophetically informed the wayward seaport residents of Corinth circa 51 AD: "The last enemy to be destroyed is death."

LT was right, Bone-rack was righteous, but it was not an accolade that Bone-rack would ever accept in his lifetime.

**Camp Reasoner, Da Nang, Vietnam circa
1970 (Bottom) and now (above).**

MARS Station, N0EFB, Da Nang, Vietnam, circa 1970. Note air conditioners in wall.

N0EFB, Da Nang operating position with "Collins S-line" and amplifier, circa 1970.

**Then state-of-the-art MARS Station at MCB,
Barstow, Ca. 1969 which worked daily phone
patches and message traffic from Vietnam.**

ABOUT THE AUTHOR

DaNang, Vietnam 1970

David Lee Foster, a long standing amateur radio operator (WA2BQT), served with the United States Marine Corps from 1968 through 1972 having been attached to both the First Marine Division and the First Marine Air Wing in and around Da Nang, Vietnam circa 1970 and 1971. His in-country service brought him into contact with several Northern I-Corps Marine Corps bases including those at An Hoa and Da Nang, Vietnam with Marine Corps MARS. As part of that contact, Sergeant Foster serviced elements of the First Marine Division Reconnaissance Battalion and the First Marine Air-wing.

Upon leaving the Marine Corps to return to school in 1972, Foster attended the University of Maryland at College Park, Maryland and

Hobart College in Geneva, New York and both Cornell University School of Law and Hofstra Law School. He holds a B.A. in Economics and Political Science and a J.D. in law. At the age of 50, he returned to divinity school at St. Bernard's School of Theology and Ministry in Rochester, New York earning an M. Div. degree.

A longtime trial and municipal attorney in Up-State, New York, Foster is involved with delivery of legal services to the indigent, private trial practice, and service as a municipal attorney in Geneva, New York. He is also involved with prison ministry and services to veterans.

Foster, 62, maintains homes in Geneva, New York and Key West, Florida, residing with his wife, Bonnie and is the father of four children ranging from 32 to 17.

ACKNOWLEDGEMENTS

Where to begin! A fitting and proper pause gives rise to the recollection of Sister St. Andrew, SSJ imploring me to think, feel, imagine, consume, embody, and exude the word "SWASHBUCKLING" while reading "Billy Budd"; from that modest indoctrination into the power of words I owe a debt I can never repay. Thank you and God bless you, Sr. St. Andrew for your indomitable spirit.

Humbly and with deep respect I acknowledge the real action heroes: the TRAP team "grunts" who lived, breathed, survived, fought and died in Vietnam; you will never be forgotten and I bow in deference to your courage, faithfulness, loyalty, esprit de corps, and extraordinary performance. But for you, many pilots would not have returned from that war. And to my fellow MARS operators: well done Marines; you brought joy to troubled hearts – "Semper Fi" to all of you.

A special thanks to friends like Tom Marsh who read with me, John Oughterson who prayed with me, Paul Middlebrook who relived these memories with me, Jim Keyser who critiqued me, and Mark Lord who commiserated with me. I am blessed and it is a goodness to behold such friendship; thank you all.

And last but hardly least, a special thanks to my family; they endured my mindless absence while absorbed in my writing. And to my children: this book is for you that you may know your father who loves you and your Father who loves you for all eternity; may He keep you in His light.

Made in the USA
Middletown, DE
05 February 2018